SEARCHING FOR HANNAH

SEARCHING FOR HANNAH

Joseph J. Saltarelli

Columbus, Ohio

The views and opinions expressed in this book are solely those of the author and do not reflect the views or opinions of Gatekeeper Press. Gatekeeper Press is not to be held responsible for and expressly disclaims responsibility of the content herein.

Searching for Hannah

Published by Gatekeeper Press
2167 Stringtown Rd, Suite 109
Columbus, OH 43123-2989
www.GatekeeperPress.com

The editorial work for this book is entirely the product of the author. Gatekeeper Press did not participate in and is not responsible for any aspect of this element.

Library of Congress Control Number: 2021951189

ISBN (paperback): 9781662917677
eISBN: 9781662917684

To Lisa, the love of my life,
for all the reasons she knows.
And to Jackie, Anthony, and Annie,
the three stars in the firmament
we created together.

Prologue

Never Give All the Heart

Never give all the heart, for love
Will hardly seem worth thinking of
To passionate women if it seem
Certain, and they never dream
That it fades out from kiss to kiss;
For everything that's lovely is
But a brief, dreamy, kind delight.
O never give the heart outright,
For they, for all smooth lips can say,
Have given their hearts up to the play.
And who could play it well enough
If deaf and dumb and blind with love?
He that made this knows all the cost,
For he gave all his heart and lost.

W.B. Yeats

If I knew that it was possible to save all the children in Germany by transporting them to England, but only half of them by transporting them to Palestine, I would choose the second—because we face not only the reckoning of those children, but the historical reckoning of the Jewish people.

David Ben-Gurion
December 1938

Reminiscing about it now, more than three decades later and with the news of Ruth's recent passing, only weeks after my last visit with her, I admit the series of events seem the oddest of coincidences. And yet, sometimes I wonder if the old adage—there are no coincidences—might well be true, that maybe, just maybe, as Ruth always said, everything that happens is meant to be.

By that June day in 1990, it already had been years since I'd spoken to Hannah. I had heard she'd gotten married two years after making aliyah to Israel in 1983, but I never learned her husband's name or whether there were children. I could say we'd lost track of each other by then, but to be honest we hadn't stayed in touch after our breakup. I imagine that's the way it is with most relationships that don't last. I wasn't sure if Hannah was still living in Israel or had moved back to New Jersey. If someone had asked me, I couldn't have told them whether she was dead or alive.

~~~

It's hard to know _why_ we remember the things we do, or whether _what_ we remember is the way things really were. All we can say is _how_ we remember what happened. It seems fair to say, too, that stories of unrequited love often begin, like this one does, with a sort of fateful fortuity. Before long, you can think of little else but the person you have come to love more than anything, but who you never can be quite sure loves you in the same way. You share countless meals together, bare your souls during long walks in the park, and steal kisses when they're least expected. In the sultry afternoons of summer and on snowbound winter nights, you give yourselves over to passions that, in each moment, seem incomparable to any that either one of you has known before. Then, suddenly, the road you're traveling together diverges, and each of you embark on a separate path to a different place. The story ends, often with far less clarity than how it began—"indeterminacy" as Hannah might say.

The years pass, new wounds are inflicted and borne, old ones heal and are mostly forgotten, until, like an unexpected gust of wind that stirs up a cluster of fallen leaves, memory carries you to another place and time, to the beginning.

Part One

1990

Chapter One

That day in June when I lost my job started out like any other. I woke early, showered, ate the same breakfast cereal I always did, and walked the five blocks from my apartment building to the subway station at 110th Street and Broadway. I caught the train uptown, got off at 238th Street in the Bronx, then took the bus over to Xavier Academy, the Catholic high school I'd attended years before. I arrived in time for homeroom bell at 8:00 a.m.

An hour later, I was lecturing on the letters of St. Paul to the small group of bleary-eyed seniors who had been brave enough to enroll in my course, Jesus in History. It was the only elective I'd been able to wrangle approval for at Xavier. It was my second year teaching it.

At the bell, Pat—Father Patrick Callaghan, a friend since high school and now Xavier's dean of academic standards—was waiting for me outside my second floor classroom. He came in just as the last student left and handed me one of two copies he had of the assignment I'd given my students the week before:

> I, Paul, of the City of Tarsus, a Hebrew born of Hebrews according to the law, send you this greeting. How is it that I came to be a follower of Jesus? I, who persecuted his followers in Jerusalem and beyond, even unto Damascus, where I had my fateful encounter with our risen Lord. Friends in Christ, many of you have asked this question of me and I have not, for these ten years, answered you in all truthfulness. In my next letter I shall answer, and tell you of my own role in our Lord's crucifixion.
> (Final assignment is to write Paul's "next letter" (30% of grade)).

"Hello Pat, to what do I owe . . ."

Pat interrupted me and proceeded to read from the paper in his hand.

"My own role in our Lord's crucifixion?" he asked sarcastically. Pat looked straight at me. "What role Michael? My God, what were you thinking when you handed this out last week?"

Pat's visit and questions were both unexpected and I was startled. "Nothing for you and the head office to get so worked up about," I replied, defensively. "I'm asking my students to use what they've learned this term and apply some critical thinking, and maybe a little poetic license. Isn't that what a college preparatory education is supposed to be about? Not a big deal. As for the prompt, they're all graduating seniors so they should be able to handle it without lapsing."

"Michael, you know exactly what I'm talking about. First of all, there isn't any *goddamn* . . ." Pat paused, correcting himself.

"Michael," he continued a moment later, "you know better than anyone there isn't any proof Paul met Jesus, much less played a role in his crucifixion. For chrissakes you're asking these Catholic school kids, whose Catholic parents are paying lots of money to send them to Catholic school, to write a fiction paper for a history of religion class. And please don't get me started on the theological aspects of it." Pat stressed the word "Catholic" all three times, as if I wasn't well aware of who signed my paychecks.

"Pat, wait, we've discussed this before, remember?" I was pleading a case that already had been lost.

Pat gave me the most dour look I'd seen in sixteen years of knowing him.

"Michael, I tried with the Big Man. I really did. But he's made up his mind this time."

The "Big Man" was Monsignor James Brennan, Xavier's principal and chief administrator. Sporting a shock of finely combed grey hair that never appeared mussed, the portly Monsignor was no fan of mine. He quizzed me regularly in the faculty lounge about aspects of Church doctrine, and had denied my requests to approve Jesus in History as a senior elective three times. He relented only after receiving Pat's informal imprimatur, albeit on condition that the course adhere strictly to Catholic orthodoxy.

"Look, I know you've saved my ass before," I said. I realized that my straying from Brennan's condition had placed Pat in a difficult spot for having vouched for me and the course syllabus.

"I get that I'm on thin ice here. I'm on a year-to-year and there's no guarantee they'll sign me on for another. You know how grateful . . ."

"Michael, . . ."

"Pat, are you saying what I think you're saying?"

Pat proceeded to tell me that the school was on track to lose students in the upcoming year, the budget needed to be adjusted accordingly, evaluations had been underway about contract renewals, there were more than enough religion teachers, and because I lacked any qualification to teach Pre-Calculus, for which there was a genuine need—and, oh if I knew anyone interested I should let Pat know—the decision had been made not to renew my contract. No, Pat said, he wasn't aware of anyone else who hadn't had their contract renewed.

I couldn't blame Pat, of course. He was a faithful friend who'd rescued me from Brennan's clutches on numerous occasions since I began teaching at Xavier. In fact, Pat was the reason I'd landed the job in the first place four years earlier, shortly after having been persuaded by my faculty adviser at Columbia University to take a leave of absence from the doctoral program in religious studies to avoid being placed on probation or, worse, asked to withdraw.

I was desperate not to have to move back to my parents' house in the Bronx, and was looking for a job so that I could continue living in the single room I rented from Dick Gorman, a lifer career counselor over at Columbia College. As a newly-minted member of Xavier's Department of Religion, Pat had started teaching at Xavier a year before while working on his dissertation at Fordham University, a tome on St. Augustine's rejection of Manichean Dualism that eventually would be published by Catholic University of America Press.

Brennan had been smitten by Pat, and was so impressed with the caliber of his intellect that Pat was able to convince him to hire me for a backup spot to teach religion and history that had just opened up due to a teacher's unexpected resignation. He told Brennan my scholarly work at Columbia was likely to "chart new territory" in Pauline studies, but that my dissertation had been sidetracked temporarily due to "family issues." Both statements were categorical violations of the Ninth Commandment.

Having carried out his mission to inform me of Brennan's decision, Pat cracked a smile, but didn't have much else to say other than that Brennan would be contacting me directly; the Big Man had wanted Pat to break the news to me informally, as we were old friends and all. I imagine losing my job was probably inevitable given how Brennan felt about me and the fact that Pat, my guardian angel at Xavier, already had accepted a position as assistant professor of theology at The Catholic University in Washington, D.C., starting in the fall. Pat mumbled something about getting together for dinner, to which I nodded silent assent, and then headed back to his third floor office.

My next class of the week, a sophomore-year survey course on European history, was scheduled to start at two o'clock that afternoon. After a half-eaten lunch, I managed to regurgitate one of my largely canned lectures on the rise of fascism in Europe and the events leading to the outbreak of the Second World War, collected the extra copies of my apparently heretical essay assignment, and left.

Chapter Two

I had no desire to linger at Xavier, and preferred to return to Manhattan as quickly as possible. The single room I rented from old Gorman was nothing more than the "maid's quarters" in a dusty, two-bedroom apartment that hadn't been redecorated in years. The building was pre-war and certainly had character, but Gorman and his wife Iris, a concert violinist, were close to retirement and, for that reason I assumed, hadn't been willing to put much money into the place. The apartment was also rent-controlled, and so my rent probably covered all of theirs, despite the fact I occupied a fraction of the space. But, in fairness, the Gormans always told me I should feel free to use the living and dining rooms, and I threw a decent party for friends there on a few occasions.

Dick and I got along "splendidly" as he liked to say, and so while he typically rented the room for three or at most four years at a time, usually to doctoral or law students, he was happy to keep me on after I had taken a leave of absence. I had thought of moving plenty of times, and even searched for a new place, but for two hundred and fifty dollars—Dick and Iris had only raised my rent by one hundred dollars since I first moved in eight years before, when I started at Columbia—it was hundreds less than most apartment shares on the Upper West Side.

The Gormans owned a small farmhouse about two hours' drive away in upstate New York, not far from the Berkshires. I hardly ever saw Iris during the week since she lived at the farmhouse, and she and Dick spent most weekends there together. On the few occasions Iris was in the city, I'd see her briefly in the evenings when, after dinner, she would take to playing mournful sonatas in the living room.

Dick was scrawny and tall, but in contrast to Iris, a mostly jovial fellow who enjoyed regaling me with proverbs in the original Latin and Greek that, he would lament, conveyed "wisdom lost to us" in the modern age. He otherwise kept to himself during the week, although I became familiar with his daily rituals such as a half-hour nap before dinner at seven. It was always preceded by a shower, after which he'd scamper, sometimes chuckling to himself but invariably stark naked, out of the bathroom and into the bedroom he shared, if only occasionally, with Iris.

I can't recall the name of the town where Dick and Iris had their country home, although they invited me several times and I visited once, with Hannah. The house was small and run down, but the location was picturesque—a flat, open meadow surrounded on three sides by thick, isolating groves of oak, pine, and sugar maple trees. After a nice lunch of sandwiches accompanied by vegetables from the Gormans' garden, Dick pulled me off to the side while Hannah was helping Iris in the kitchen, whence he explained how impressed he was with Hannah's "smarts" and social charms, and offered me the proverbial advice, "Don't let this one get away Michael." I assured Dick that I had no intention of doing so.

It took a bit longer than usual to get back to 110th Street, and after arriving I didn't feel like going straight to the apartment so I meandered down Broadway, browsing in a few bookshops and music stores. I recall it being a lovely day, sunny and mild, with a cool breeze that reminded me of that Saturday afternoon Hannah and I spent at the Cloisters Museum. As it got closer to seven, I decided to stop at Dimitri's, the diner at the corner of 107th Street and Broadway where I often grabbed dinner and almost always ate breakfast on Sunday mornings.

I remember one such Sunday morning in October 1982, the day after our visit to the Cloisters. Hannah and I were having breakfast in one of the red leather booths at Dimitri's—right side of the double row, second in from the front. Holding Hannah's hands in mine, I repeated what I had told her the night before for the first time, that I had fallen "crazy in love" with her. Hannah leaned forward and, clutching with her right hand the necklace I'd given her the previous night as a birthday gift, whispered "me too." Then, without skipping a beat she waved down the passing waiter and barked out an order for Challah French Toast with strawberries and her favorite drink, hot tea with lemon. We laughed, and kissed, then laughed again.

Entering Dimitri's that evening in June 1990, however, I wasn't thinking of Hannah. I was thinking, instead, of Estrella, a waitress from the Dominican Republic who I found attractive and had gotten to know. Estrella lived in Washington Heights, a short subway ride away. Having decided in her mid-twenties to return to school and obtain her degree, she was working full-time at Dimitri's while attending Hunter College, where she majored in social work. She'd been married at an early age following high school, but had since divorced. She was living with her parents and helped care for her disabled father. Despite these burdens Estrella was invariably light-hearted and cheerful, a sunny disposition I found appealing if only because it was in marked contrast to my generally gloomy one.

Estrella was talking to another customer when she saw me and raised her hand slightly to wave. She liked to chat with me about her family, co-workers, the day's zanier patrons, just about anything that came to mind.

Estrella always made sure to take my order when I came in asking for a table and, to be honest, I'd started looking out for her myself. The first time we met she'd explained that her name means "star" in Spanish and is pronounced "Es-tray-uh." I had formed a habit of calling her back to ask for "one more thing," a way of extending our conversation, and she had one of winking at me whenever she finished talking. We'd been flirting with each other like that for a few months, although nothing had come of it. I wasn't quite sure why. Seeing her, though, reminded me of the promise I'd made two weeks before to take her for a drink one night after her shift ended.

Having just been fired from Xavier, however, I was in no mood for small talk. I avoided direct eye contact with Estrella, and headed straight for the counter where I ordered a chicken salad sandwich and fries to go. I lived a few minutes' walk from Dimitri's, on the corner of 105th and Riverside Drive.

The Gormans' apartment was on the eighth floor. It was Wednesday night and Dick was usually home by the time I arrived, but he appeared to have gone out. I put the bag with my sandwich on the table in the kitchen, which was off to the left of the living room as you entered the apartment, and headed to my room.

After first moving into the apartment back in 1982, it had taken a bit of convincing but Dick agreed to install a separate telephone line for me. I hated having to give friends and family the Gormans' number if they needed to call me, or to use their phone to call them. This was long before the era of social media, cell phones, and texting, and back then everyone used landlines or public telephones to talk to other people. Once Dick had the phone hooked up, I bought an answering machine. The phone and machine were on a small nightstand at the head of my bed, near the window where the phone jack had to be installed.

Perhaps because I was distracted by what had happened that day, I didn't notice the flashing light indicating there were messages. I was drawn instead to the pile of books and papers strewn about the opposite corner of the room, at the foot of the bed. Among them were the 438 pages of an unfinished dissertation on the first-century split between Pharisees and Sadducees concerning the belief in life after death, which had taken as its starting point Paul's trial before Festus, described in Acts 25-27.

Paul had famously declared he was on trial because of his belief in the resurrection of the dead. But Acts 26 v.4 was the passage that intrigued me.

That's where Paul tells Agrippa that the Jews "know my way of life from my youth, a life spent from the beginning among my own people and in Jerusalem." I interpreted the passage to suggest that Paul, a Pharisee, might have known Jesus, perhaps played a role in his crucifixion, even further, that Paul's testimony to Jesus' resurrection was part of the broader theological and political struggle between Pharisees and Sadducees. There wasn't much scholarly support for that unconventional view—essentially none, in fact—but Pat and I had consumed quite a few bottles of Chianti arguing the point. There were times Pat got drunk enough I had him nearly convinced.

My dissertation was another matter. It remained a garbled mess, and I had never been able to form a coherent thesis statement much less marshal sufficient evidence and arguments to support it. So I shouldn't have been surprised when Professor Wertheimer, my dissertation adviser, told me after reviewing an early draft that I appeared to have more promise as a "historical fiction novelist" than as a scholar of primitive Christianity. Not long afterward it was "recommended" that I take a leave of absence from the program.

~~~

I was starting to get hungry. After washing the metaphorical debris of the day from my face I headed out toward the kitchen. It was only then that I noticed the flashing number "2" on the answering machine. I walked over and pressed the play button.

"Hello, Michael, I think this is the right number, but you mustn't be home." It was an older woman's voice, a bit halting and nervous sounding, but familiar.

"Michael, this is Ruth Lindemann, Hannah's mom."

I gripped the side of the nightstand.

"It's been a very long time since we've spoken, and I don't know if you ever expected to hear my voice again. But, please, call me if you get this message."

There was a short pause. "It's about Hannah."

I stood in disbelief as the machine skipped to the second message. It was Ruth again. She'd forgotten to leave her number, which was the same as I had remembered it. Ruth wasn't sure, she said, whether I would have.

Chapter Three

I slept late the next morning. I didn't have classes scheduled, and although required to show up at Xavier regardless, no one was likely to notice or care about my absence, especially so close to the end of the school year. I was even less likely to care now that my contract wasn't going to be renewed. I hadn't called Ruth back, and still wasn't sure whether I would. I lay in bed for an hour wondering what it was she wanted to tell me about Hannah.

I had never eaten my sandwich from the night before and the bag was still on the kitchen table, emitting an awful stench. I threw it away and decided on the fly to head up to the old neighborhood in the Bronx, where it all began seventeen years before. I thought a visit might clear my head and help me to decide what to do. To get there from Columbia, I needed to take the subway downtown to Times Square, the shuttle across to Grand Central Terminal, then the subway uptown to Burke Avenue, where Zelda's Hat Shop had been all those years ago.

After getting off the train, I walked down Burke toward Willow Tree Lane, the street I grew up on, which was lined with mostly single and two-family homes. Although the neighborhood seemed much the same, many of the Irish, Italian, and German families had migrated to the northern suburbs, as had my father, who had moved to a house in Westchester, close to one of my sisters, a few years after my mother's death. Those who already had been on in years when I was growing up had likely passed away, the Italians waked at Califano's on Crosby, and the Irish at Halloran's on Roberts.

Dom's Italian Bakery was there on Burke, as always; the new owners had changed its name but everyone still called it Dom's. Across the street, on the other side of the "El"—the elevated No. 6 train line that hovered over Westchester Avenue like a spark-sputtering snake—Sellinger's Clothing Emporium was now a Spanish bodega, old Sellinger having dropped to the floor dead nearly fifteen years before. Continuing to walk north on Burke, I noticed that Krenshaw's Meat Market had been converted into a five-and-dime, and Yorktown Savings into a florist shop. Abe, the ever-comical, diehard Yankees fan who made the best egg creams in the Bronx, had long since retired to Florida after selling Honest Abe's candy store to a middle-aged Pakistani couple. They were still using his sign with the penny portrait of

President Lincoln. Steve's Variety Store was a corner deli run by a Greek family.

I crossed the street to where Zelda's Hat Shop had been, the space now occupied by Vince's Electronics Repair. The shop seemed even smaller than I had remembered. Looking through the store window all I could see was a cluttered customer counter with cash register and mounds of assemblies, loose wires, and television tubes scattered about. Gone were the carefully organized table displays stacked with clothes, and the neat rows of shelves brimming over with hats, scarves, gloves, pocketbooks, and other accessories that had lined the side and back walls when Zelda ran the place.

I walked up to the door and, squinting, noticed traces of black soot on the bricks just above the door jamb. A moment later, a burly man, who I presumed to be Vince, opened the door and asked me what I was doing and if I needed help with anything. I said no, that I was looking around the neighborhood I had grown up in, and remembered that his store had been an old woman's hat shop before it burned down in 1973, on Christmas Day. He motioned for me to enter.

"Christmas Day! Don't know nothing about that," he said. "But 1973, that was a long time ago, seventeen years. I've been renting this place for six years and never heard about the fire. Owner never told me anything. I just hope it doesn't bring me bad luck in my seventh year." I couldn't tell whether he was serious, but said I was sure it wouldn't. He invited me to look around and I did for a few minutes, almost tripping over a giant TV tube assembly on the tiled floor. As I was preparing to leave I thanked him for his kindness; he looked up from behind the counter and said, "I hope you find what you came looking for." I smiled, nodded my head, and left.

I continued down the street past the four-story apartment building where Zelda lived for decades, stopping in front of the Jewish Center of Pelham Bay, which I walked past every day for eight years on my way to school. The metal gate was padlocked, but the sign in front listed the regular times of Friday evening and Saturday morning services. I walked to the corner, turned, and followed Burke till it intersected with Bruckner Boulevard, passing on the way my family's old house on Willow Tree Lane. I crossed the walkway spanning Interstate 95 to Pelham Bay Park, the same one I'd crossed countless times before.

Pelham Bay Park, the largest park in New York City and where I spent so much of my boyhood, had a storied history of its own. During the Revolutionary War, it was the site of the famous Battle of Pell's Point, the name of the area at the time. George Washington and the main portion of the Continental Army were positioned up in Harlem Heights, in Manhattan, following the British invasion and occupation of Long Island. With British forces pressing Washington from the south and hoping to cut off his means of escape, British General William Howe landed his troops at Pell's Point, where they were beaten back by a much smaller force of Continental soldiers under the command of Colonel John Glover. The resulting delay allowed Washington and his forces to escape northward to White Plains, saving the Continental Army and possibly altering the course of the war.

Once in the park, I continued past the noisy, always-crowded playground and through the quiet, sylvan fields down to the bay, where that summer, sixteen summers before, I sat cross-legged on the rocks staring at the water and thinking about the girl with curly brown hair who, I thought, I'd never see again. There, sitting at that same spot overlooking the bay, and compelled by a mixture of memory, curiosity, and concern, I decided I would call Ruth as soon as I got back to the apartment.

Part Two

1973 - 1974

Chapter Four

I learned about the Yom Kippur War while watching Walter Cronkite on the CBS Evening News. Cronkite's report was the first time I'd heard anything about the conflict between Jews and Arabs in the Middle East. A few weeks later Saudi Arabia announced the Arab oil boycott, and by late-November the price of a barrel of oil had risen from three dollars to twelve dollars.

Fascinated by these events in the far-off and exotic Middle East, I took it upon myself to write a little piece about the war and submitted it to Sister Mary Clare for the December edition of the school's monthly newsletter, which the sisters in the front office printed using one of those old-fashioned mimeograph machines, the kind with the purplish-blue ink and intoxicating smell that ended up smudging whole sections of text and leaving the paper soggy. I felt a measure of pride when Sister Mary Clare placed my single, somewhat too-long paragraph as lead article in the newsletter, just above the reminder about St. Regina's annual Christmas fair.

With lines stretching for blocks forming at the Gulf station, and with the price of gas continuing to rise, Sister Mary Clare brought up the war in our daily religion class.

"This war is between Jews and Moslems," she inveighed at us. "It has nothing to do with our country, but the Arabs are raising the price of gas because we helped the Jews win the war.

"Remember, Jews do not believe in Jesus Christ. They *crucified* him," she scowled, emphasizing the first syllable of the word crucified. "And Moslems *hate* us Catholics. Every Moslem is taught that he'll go to Heaven if he kills a Catholic."

~~~

Exactly one week before Christmas, Sister June Francis told us we had to bring a styrofoam ball to art class the very next day. We would decorate and take it home as a Christmas tree ornament. My mother had no idea what styrofoam was, but gave me about a dollar fifty's worth of change and told me to try Steve's Variety Store.

It was cold, sleeting, and already dark when I set out for Steve's, which was on the corner of Burke and Hobart Avenues directly across the street from Zelda's shop. Steve could be a gruff man on the best of occasions and that evening was no exception. I repeated what Sister June Francis had told us.

"You're the fifth kid come in today asking me for that," Steve growled. "Like I told them I'm telling you, I don't carry it." Annoyed, he turned to deal with an adult customer looking to buy an extension cord for his Christmas lights.

As I left Steve's, I happened to look across the street at Zelda's shop. Due to increased electricity bills resulting from the boycott, local merchants had skipped the Christmas lights they normally hung, and shared payment for each year, and the streets were only dimly lit by the city lampposts.

Just at that moment the sight of a young girl outside the hat shop caught my eye. She was standing in front of the store, and appeared to be helping guide Zelda, still inside, to position a Menorah in the lower left corner of the window display, across from the glowing, small white Christmas tree on the opposite side. It was Tuesday and the following evening would be the first night of Hanukkah, the eight-day Festival of Lights that I had always heard described as the "Jewish Christmas."

Like others in the neighborhood, my mother visited Zelda's throughout the year to buy house clothes or the occasional, last-minute gift and, at Easter, new hats for my sisters. When I accompanied her on those visits, Zelda appeared to be in her sixties, frail and a bit obese, with unkempt gray hair. She walked with a slight limp favoring her left leg, and spoke with an unfamiliar accent whose origin I couldn't discern at the time, but later learned was German.

I remember my mother haggling with Zelda on those Easter visits, insisting on a better price since she was buying not one but three hats. Inevitability, a deal would be struck. But at that point in time I hadn't been inside Zelda's shop for a while, as my sisters, all older than me and in high school, no longer wore hats on Easter Sunday the way they had when they were younger.

As Zelda was locking the front door, the girl turned and appeared to notice me. For a brief moment we stared at each other across the slushy street, our views interrupted by passing cars or the occasional, lumbering truck making a last delivery of the day. When Zelda finished locking up, she took the girl's hand and they started walking down the avenue.

I was soaked and shivering by the time the two of them turned the corner, but I still needed to find a store that had styrofoam balls. On a hunch I walked two blocks up to Crosby, where a drug store had opened recently. I remembered from an earlier visit that the store had Christmas paper and decorations. There were a handful of the balls left, and I bought the largest I could afford with the change in my pocket. It wasn't three inches but would have to do.

~~~

In a roundabout sort of way, it was my friend Louis who introduced me to Hannah. Louis was living in the house across the street, with his father and two sisters. I remember how years earlier, after long, sweaty afternoons of play, Louis' mother would invite me to the apartment with him to taste some of the things she'd made for dinner. The last occasion had been a chilly, late-autumn evening three years before when, with her typically ebullient smile, she proudly displayed to us a dish filled with fresh-cut, slimy frog's legs she was about to bread and fry up in the pan. Hiding my grimace as best I could, and no doubt to her disappointment, I concocted some excuse not to wait around to enjoy one. I'd next see her only a little more than a year later, laid out at Califano's, resplendent in a cream-colored, lace-embroidered gown, her auburn hair coiffed and forever still, taken in the prime of life by the same aggressive cancer that would claim my own mother a decade on. It was the first time I witnessed death. In genuflection on the velveted casket kneeler, my hands joined in outwardly pious but mock prayer and with Louis and his father dutifully standing sentry nearby, I stared at her face, spellbound by the made-over visage projecting an illusion of serene sleep—handiwork of what our neighbor the curmudgeonly Alphonse "the Gout" would refer to as the "mortician's magic."

After school most days Louis and I would play stickball or touch football, or race each other to the fire hydrant in front of the O'Connors' house. Louis was a great sprinter and always beat me. We couldn't play handball in winter because the Spaldeens we used got too hard in the cold air and would hurt our hands. But during the three other seasons we played all the time against the wall of the apartment building next to Louis' house, except when the super put the garbage cans out and they blocked the third square of the sidewalk closest to the street. On that Saturday before Christmas in 1973, it was too cold to play anything, so Louis and I were bored and just passing time on my front stoop.

Louis attended P.S. 71, the public school on Roberts Avenue a few blocks away. He had in the past mentioned to me that a girl our age had moved down the street the previous summer and went to the same school he did. I assumed she might be the girl I'd seen helping Zelda close the shop a few days before, and I decided to casually ask Louis about her.

"They're Jewish," Louis blurted out. "My father says the dad works at the UN or something. He said Jews are to blame for the gas lines. He waited two and a half hours the other day, and then there was none left."

"But what's the girl's name?" I asked, trying my best to sound ambivalent.

"Hannah something. I don't know her last name. She's kind of weird, though, a bookworm type," Louis replied. "Why, you like her?" he asked next in a self-congratulatory tone, apparently concluding he had uncovered the real reason for my question. I said nothing in response, and immediately challenged him to a race down to the O'Connors' house, winter coats and all.

I lost.

Chapter Five

No one knew how the fire started. All I remember is waking up Christmas morning to the sound of sirens shortly before dawn. My sister and I rushed to the living room, which was in the front of the rectangular-shaped apartment and faced out onto Willow Tree Lane. My mother was already there, her head perched out the window despite the cold. We couldn't see the fire trucks but they were close.

A couple of hours later, after my father had enjoyed his morning espresso and breakfast of Stella D'oro cookies, I went with him to buy bread from Dom's Bakery, which was on Burke Avenue close to the station. One fire truck was still there, parked in front of Zelda's shop. The storefront glass had been shattered, and the bricks above were blackened by soot; lingering smoke continued to seep out of the place. From what I could tell the shop had been completely gutted.

Zelda was standing at the edge of the sidewalk, a blanket draped over her shoulders. She was holding a charred Menorah and its dangling electrical cord in her hands. Next to her were a man and a woman who both appeared to be in their late-thirties, and the girl I'd seen the week before and later learned was Hannah. For the whole time my father and I watched she never once left Zelda's side.

~~~

I saw Hannah a few times that winter, but always from a distance. She would be walking on the other side of the street, where she lived, sometimes with her mother, sometimes alone. I'd always look at her when she passed by and we'd make eye contact. One time, I thought she waved at me with the slightest movement of her hand, so slight I could tell her mother hadn't noticed.

I finally spoke to Hannah for the first, and what I thought would be the last time, in April, on Good Friday to be exact. I was sitting alone on the front stoop of our house, and saw Hannah walking in my direction. I was surprised since I'd never seen her walk on my side of the street before. As she approached, our eyes met and my heart started racing. I gritted my teeth and clenched my fist in frustration, trying anxiously to think of something catchy to say as she walked past. But, then, she suddenly stopped and spoke to me.

"Hi, I'm Hannah," she said, her voice assertive and firm.

"Hi, . . . my name is . . . I'm, . . . I'm Michael," I stammered in reply.

Hannah said she remembered seeing me on Christmas morning, after the fire. She told me that Zelda was her grandmother.

"I'm really sorry about the fire. When is your grandmother gonna reopen the store?"

"It's closed for good," Hannah replied. "She's moving to New Jersey with us as soon as the school year is over."

"But, didn't you just move here?" I asked, remembering what Louis had told me.

"Last summer, but my father said he's had it with this neighborhood and decided we should leave. He said it was a mistake coming here."

My heart sank. The momentary excitement at Hannah's stopping to speak to me, along with the hope we'd see each other again over the summer, had all been dashed. I wanted to keep the conversation going, but was too nervous to ask about the fire, and too naive to ask what it was about the neighborhood that her father didn't like anymore.

Breaking the awkward silence, Hannah asked me, "Do you know what all that screaming on the street was about before?"

I had witnessed the commotion earlier and proceeded to tell Hannah about the second, third, and fourth-hand rumors I'd heard. At the Veneration of the Cross service at Annunciation Church, a woman praying at the side altar near the statue of Mary had suddenly started shouting that she'd seen blood streaming down the Blessed Mother's face. Before long she'd run out of the Church followed by several other agitated parishioners who were also claiming to have witnessed the "miracle." Within minutes, as the Church emptied and then began to fill up again with the curious, myself included, another woman was telling people on the street that she'd heard someone else had seen Jesus descend from the cross and run down the center aisle. The hullabaloo had begun to subside only a few minutes before Hannah crossed my path. Years later, I would recognize the bizarre incident for what it had been: a fairly common example of mass hysteria induced by the purported sighting of Marian tears. But, back then, I was fourteen and not yet out of grade school; I hardly knew what to make of it.

"When *you* went to the Church did *you* see anything," Hannah asked me skeptically.

"No, nothing. Only the priest and a bunch of people sitting in the pews."

"You don't believe any of that happened, do you?"

"Well, no, not really. I did think it was kind of scary though." The image I'd formed of the statue of Jesus becoming animated, jumping off the cross, and running wildly down the aisle in his loincloth seemed almost demonic, reminding me of the movie *The Exorcist*, which I'd gone to see with Louis and his father only a few months before.

"Why, are you afraid of Jesus?"

"Not when he's up on the cross. But if I saw him jump off and start running toward me, I would be. I'd start running as fast as I could."

Hannah and I giggled, and I was happy that I'd succeeded in making her laugh. A moment later, she sat down next to me.

"You know," Hannah said, "I like the city much better than this place." Everyone I knew who lived in the Bronx—Hannah was no exception—seemed to refer to Manhattan only as "the city." Other than my solitary visit to the Empire State Building, I had no point of comparison. Hannah talked about how different it was living and going to school in Manhattan, with restaurants, museums, and Central Park. She missed those things, and now would be moving to a "boring suburb." She told me about some books she'd been reading, and I remember her mentioning Pearl S. Buck's, *The Good Earth*, which I wouldn't read until high school. I listened mostly, struck by Hannah's confident air and the ease with which she spoke to me as if we had known each other for years, despite the fact we'd only just met.

After almost an hour had passed, Hannah stood up and announced that she had to leave. She was on her way to visit her grandmother who lived in the apartment building on the corner of Burke and Mahan Avenues, a few hundred feet from the hat shop and right next door to the Jewish Center of Pelham Bay. In addition to being Good Friday, it was also the last night of Passover, Hannah told me.

"We're Jewish, and I have to help my grandmother get ready for Shabbos," Hannah said, using a word I'd never heard before.

"I know," I said.

"You know I have to help my grandmother with Shabbos dinner?" Hannah asked, sounding incredulous.

"No," I said, "I know that you're Jewish."

"Well, some of the boys around here are real jerks about it."

"I'm not a jerk about it," I said.

Hannah told me she hadn't thought so, but needed to go because she was already very late and there was still cooking to do and last-minute preparations to help her grandmother with. I asked Hannah about Shabbos, and she explained its meaning to me and described how her family observed it. Hannah wished me luck in high school and said goodbye, waving her hand in a rapid motion from left to right. She began walking away, then abruptly turned and approached me again. I stood up in response to her gesture, but before I could say anything she leaned forward and kissed me, quickly on my cheek, then nervously said goodbye again and left.

I still had never kissed a girl, but that day was the first time I'd been kissed by one. It lasted for only a second, but its effects would linger for years.

~~~

I learned about the Holocaust two weeks after meeting Hannah. At the end of April, ABC aired *QB VII*, a two-part movie adaptation of Leon Uris' novel of the same name. I was captivated by the descriptions of the medical experiments that had been performed on Jewish prisoners in the "Jadwiga" concentration camp, and by the trial scene in which the lawyer, played by Anthony Quayle, cross-examines Dr. Adam Kelno, the camp doctor portrayed by Anthony Hopkins.

Kelno is asked about the significance of the letter "J" written next to prisoners' names on camp medical records. Pressed to repeat his answer so the judge and jury could hear him, Kelno shouts out "Jew" to the stunned courtroom. I found the scene riveting and couldn't get it out of my mind. The movie influenced my thinking about the Holocaust for years.

I knew about the Second World War from my encyclopedia reading, as well as the stories told by my parents about the fierce fighting they witnessed, and suffering they endured, in their small town in Italy following the Allied invasion in 1943. But prior to watching *QB VII*, I had been largely unaware of what happened in the concentration camps. For weeks afterward I lay awake at night, troubled and unable to sleep. I thought about Hannah and Zelda, and the fact they were Jewish, about the Christmas fire, and about how for years the only thing we'd been taught in St. Regina about Jews was that they had "killed Jesus." But mostly, I thought about Hannah and felt sad she was moving away.

Never in a million years did I expect to see her again.

1982 - 1983

Chapter Six

The Official Delegation of the Government of
Lebanon invites you to a cocktail reception in
celebration of the UN General Assembly.
Please join us in Room 309 of the
Princeton Holiday Inn, beginning at 9:00 p.m.
Refreshments and *hor d'oeuvres* will be served.

A s the head of NYU's Model UN delegation
representing the fractured State of Lebanon, I
circulated the flyers in each of the conference
rooms where our meetings had been held. Thanks to
the largesse of NYU we had enough money to cover
hotel and meal charges, and plenty left over to buy
supplies of beer, vodka, gin, and various sodas and
snacks. If the 1982 party was anything like the one we
had thrown the prior year, when the conference had
been hosted at Georgetown, the night was going to be
another success. I was particularly looking forward
to it because I had something else to celebrate; I was
graduating that year.

Adjoining rooms 309 and 311 of the Princeton Holiday Inn were ready by nine, as promised, but like most college parties ours didn't get started until ten. Before long, we had twenty or so students from five or six schools in attendance. I was single-mindedly on the lookout for Jillian, a rather voluptuous senior at the University of Pennsylvania with whom I'd struck up a conversation earlier in the day. Jillian had been chatting with other students in one of the meeting rooms in which I'd chosen to drop off our flyers. Probably sensing she'd become the object of my gaze, she broke away from the others to ask what the flyers were about. I promptly invited her to our party and encouraged her to bring along all of her friends.

By eleven, Jillian and I had had a few drinks and found ourselves nestled in one of the corner chairs, our lips locked together. Pausing for a moment and pulling away, Jillian blurted out, "I'm supposed to tell you my friend wants to meet you. She says she knows you. Her name is Hannah Lindemann."

Whether it was the gin or my fixation on Jillian's dazzling red hair, it took a moment for her reference to Hannah to register. When it did I asked Jillian which of her friends she was talking about, and she pointed to a petite woman in the corner of the room, glass in hand, who was looking over at us. Hannah hadn't come to the party with Jillian, who I intercepted as soon as she walked through the door, and I must have missed her arrival as I was already engaged with Jillian by then. Hannah had seen me earlier in the day during one of the sessions, Jillian said. She told Jillian she recognized and wanted to meet me after Jillian mentioned my invitation to the party.

Jillian got up from the chair and led me by the hand to the other side of the room. "Hannah," she said, "this is Michael. Michael, this is Hannah. I believe you know each other. Now, I'm going to get myself another drink and leave this to the two of you." Hannah still had curly brown hair, fuller in the style of the times and falling on her shoulders now, and the same penetrating, deep set eyes.

"Do you remember me?" Hannah said with a smile. "I lived on Willow Tree Lane eight years ago before moving to New Jersey. My grandmother Zelda owned that hat shop on Burke Avenue.

"You know," she added, "the one that burned down."

Chapter Seven

Surprised at the serendipity of our meeting again after eight years, I listened as Hannah told me that she still lived in New Jersey, and that her father had worked at the UN for a number of years but was now an economist at one of the big banks in the city. I asked if her father's position with the UN was the reason she'd joined the Model UN Society at UPenn. She laughed and said no, it was the great things she'd heard about the NYU parties.

Although Hannah's parents were doing well, she said, Zelda had been in failing health for the last few years, some kind of heart ailment. I told Hannah my mother had passed away from cancer two years before, but that my father was still living on Willow Tree Lane. As college students always seem to do when they first meet, we asked each other about our majors. Hannah's had been comparative literature, mine, a double major in history and religion.

Fresh drinks in hand, we shared a sense of bemusement at having run into each other, even more so at the fact we'd both be attending Columbia University in the fall. I was planning to earn a master's degree in religion, my ultimate goal being a doctorate in the history of early Christianity. Hannah would be pursuing a master's degree at Teachers College, and planned to teach English literature.

By midnight our party was going strong, although a few of the "delegates" had moved on, either to other soirées or to their rooms. Nearly all of the students participating in the conference were staying at the Holiday Inn, which had grouped us on two floors and had obviously prepared for the onslaught since we never received complaints or requests from the hotel's management to shut the party down despite the noise. Just after midnight Hannah suggested we go to her room, which she was sharing with Jillian, because it was empty and we could talk more easily.

Hannah and Jillian's room was farther down the hall near the exit stairs, and as Hannah had predicted it was quiet; Jillian was still at the party chatting with Vania, one of my NYU friends originally from Brazil. Hannah and I sat on the bed and continued catching up. She asked me in a curious tone why I had decided to get a master's degree in religion.

I explained my fascination with Jesus, how as a boy I had considered the priesthood, had memorized entire scenes from the movie *The Robe*—about the Roman centurion who Pontius Pilate placed in charge of crucifying Jesus—and how I'd spent each Good Friday in my backyard re-enacting the crucifixion with a makeshift cross that I'd fashioned out of pieces of wood from my father's basement, anxiously awaiting the "ninth hour"—3:00 p.m.—at which time, according to Sister Mary Clare, Jesus "surrendered his spirit to God." It had never been the inscrutable mystery of Jesus' birth that intrigued me, I told Hannah, but, rather, the cloudy circumstances that led to his death.

"Is that what you'd been doing that Friday when we talked to each other for the first time?" Hannah asked, sounding shocked.

"No," I insisted, wondering suddenly whether I'd revealed too much information. "I was a grown man of fourteen by then," I added jokingly.

"I'm confused," Hannah said. "Do you still believe in Jesus or not?"

I was stumped by Hannah's question. It was one I'd asked myself countless times but never been asked by anyone else, at least not so directly. I told Hannah no, that I had first expressed my doubts to Father Delmonico in the confessional in eighth grade—my penance consisted of twelve Our Fathers and six Hail Marys—and fully lost my faith midway through college. No single event like the death of my mother had triggered it, I said, although having witnessed how terribly she suffered, especially at the end, might have given me cause enough. I preferred to think I had reasoned my way out of Catholicism's grip. The faith had been force-fed into me over eight years, but then over the following eight years had leaked out bit by bit until there was none left. I told Hannah about the close friendship I'd developed with Pat in high school discussing religion and philosophy, and explained that he had found something deeply sustaining in his religious faith and planned to become a priest. Having graduated from Fordham in three years, he was a first-year student at Dunwoodie Seminary in Yonkers, working on a master's degree in theology. He'd go on to earn his PhD in Theology from Fordham.

Although I no longer believed in the divinity of Jesus, I told Hannah, I'd never stopped being fascinated by him, or the history-changing movement inspired by his life, death, and, at least to his followers, resurrection. I said the turning point in my worldview of Christianity as an intellectual, if not spiritual, endeavor had been a religion course I'd taken in my sophomore year at NYU called Historical Jesus, with Professor Peter Walsh. Walsh's course had set me on the path to do graduate work in the history of early Christianity, and, a number of years later, I would model my own course at Xavier after his.

Curiously enough, it turned out Walsh had grown up in Pelham Bay in the 1940s. Over beers at McSorley's Old Ale House in the Village, Walsh explained to me how Westchester Avenue had been a border of sorts between the Italian and Irish sections of our neighborhood. Although there had been some spillover since his time—my and Louis' families were examples—the Irish had lived mostly east of the El and were parishioners of the Annunciation Church— just down the street from me—while the Italians lived west of the El and attended St. Regina.

My conversation with Walsh made me realize why Father McGuinness at Annunciation rejected my sisters year after year, and had always tried to dissuade my parents from re-applying. By the time I was ready to start school they'd gotten the message and enrolled me, without a hitch, in St. Regina, even though it meant a fifteen-minute walk to the other side of the neighborhood.

I asked Hannah whether she had ever experienced antisemitism during the time she lived in Pelham Bay. She told me there had been plenty of nasty sneers and snubs at school, especially at Christmas, and that she'd been called a "Heeb" a lot by boys on our street, making it clear Louis had been one of them. And then there was the Christmas fire. The Fire Department had concluded that the fire that destroyed Zelda's shop had been the result of arson, although no one had been prosecuted as far as Hannah knew. Hannah's father was convinced antisemitism was behind it.

Afterward, he decided to move the family, including Zelda, to New Jersey.

Hannah and her parents were observant, but not overly religious, she said. They attended synagogue on most Saturday mornings and the High Holy Days, but weren't strict about it, or about keeping kosher. While living in Pelham Bay, Zelda had attended Friday and Saturday services at the Jewish Center next door to her apartment building. Hannah told me her father was "obsessed with" Middle East affairs and a "strong supporter" of Israel.

It was now three in the morning, and Hannah and I were on the bed across from each other. Apparently not wanting to disturb us, Jillian never returned. We later learned she'd stayed the night with the two other UPenn students on her team.

As we lay on the bed, our heads propped up by our arms resting on elbows and inches apart, I leaned over and asked Hannah if I could kiss her. She smiled and said "Yes, but first tell me if you asked Jillian the same question." We both laughed, and in the moment I didn't pursue the kiss.

"I may have forgotten my manners with Jillian," I stammered.

"She seemed to have forgiven you from what I saw," Hannah replied. "That wasn't exactly part of the plan."

Now that Hannah had revealed her "plan" to meet me, my undiplomatic dalliance with her red-headed co-delegate from Mozambique wasn't something I thought wise to continue discussing.

"Tell me about your grandmother," I said, extemporizing as quickly as I could. "How did she come to live in Pelham Bay and open up a hat shop?"

"My grandmother's name is Griselda, which is German. Zelda is a sort of nickname. She was born in Munich. Her father, my great-grandfather, owned a hat factory there.

"My bubbe, . . ." Hannah paused a moment.

"Bubbe is Yiddish for grandmother. I don't always call her that but sometimes I do.

"Anyway"—Hannah enunciated the single word as "any" and "way"—"my grandmother told me stories about going to the factory after school and helping her father close up. Then they'd walk home together and she'd tell him about her day. When Hitler came to power everything changed, as I'm sure you're aware."

"Yes, heard a bit about it," I replied.

"My grandfather's name was Stefan Reiner. I never knew him because he didn't survive the war. He wasn't Jewish. He was the son of one of my great-grandfather's suppliers. He and my grandmother married in 1934, just after Hitler came to power, when it was still legal for gentiles and Jews to marry.

My mother, Ruth, was born in 1936. But as things got worse, Jews left Germany, for America, England, Palestine, wherever they could escape to. My great-grandfather wanted to leave, and my bubbe wanted to go with him, but my grandfather didn't want to leave behind his family. He and my grandmother were divorced after she applied for a visa along with my great-grandfather. My great-grandmother had died many years earlier.

"It's all a bit murky to be honest. A lot of Germans divorced Jewish spouses after Hitler took over, so I don't know whether that was the reason, or whether it was because he didn't want to leave his own family in Germany. My grandmother never wants to talk about it, and neither does my mom. I can't really blame them. My grandfather ended up in the army and was killed in 1943, fighting partisans in Yugoslavia."

"That's quite the story. Did your grandmother ever remarry?"

"No. They settled in Pelham Bay when they came to America. My great-grandfather was a broken man by then. He wanted to, but wasn't able to start a new business because he had to give most of his money to the Nazis as a fee for leaving the country. They lived together, and my bubbe later went to work in the garment district once my mom was old enough for school. She told me there'd been an influx of Germans and German Jews to the Pelham Bay area by the early

1920s, around the time the Jewish Center was built. With a little money she was able to save, she opened the hat shop a few years after my great-grandfather died. She always said it was her way to honor him. His name was Walter Manzbach."

"So your mother grew up in the apartment building on Burke Avenue next to the Jewish Center? I walked past it every day on my way to school."

I told Hannah that I hadn't known of the extensive German connection to Pelham Bay, and that her story reminded me my parents had bought their house on Willow Tree Lane in the early-1960s from a couple who had emigrated from Germany in the mid-1920s.

Hannah went on to tell me that her mother met her father while both were attending City College of New York and volunteering for Adlai Stevenson's 1956 presidential campaign. They were married in 1958, the summer after graduation. Hannah, an only child, was born in 1960, in Chicago where her father was studying for a PhD in economics at the University of Chicago. He got his first job as a research economist with ECOSOC, the United Nations Economic and Social Council, although he'd started working for a bank in the city about five years before. They had lived in Manhattan until Hannah was thirteen, when they moved to Willow Tree Lane to be closer to Zelda, who was getting older and needed help to run the shop.

It was now around 4:00 a.m., and Hannah and I agreed we had better get some sleep before the final session, which was scheduled to begin at nine in the morning. We promised to meet before leaving, and after giving me "permission this time" Hannah let me kiss her on the lips. My head was spinning by the time I crawled into bed close to five, and I wasn't sure I could sleep after what had just happened. The cyclonic snores of my "co-delegate" Gary didn't help. But before long I fell into a deep slumber.

I woke up three hours later with a pounding headache. When not fending off Gary's pestering questions about "how far" I'd gotten with Hannah—for most of the conference Gary had attempted, without success, to persuade Vania to sleep with him—I spent breakfast reflecting on Hannah's story about Zelda.

It wasn't until years later that I learned none of it was true.

Chapter Eight

The Model UN conference ended as most such affairs do, a mixture of mild disappointment and hangover fatigue. The group of us from NYU, four in total, had driven down to Princeton in my car, so I was planning to drive the other team members home, one to Manhattan and two over to Queens. I scrambled to find Hannah, who was with Jillian and her other friends from UPenn. Seeing Jillian was a bit awkward, but it helped when she made light of our brief encounter the night before. Hannah and I exchanged phone numbers, and we agreed to see each other again soon. I promised to call her that week.

Hannah was staying in a dorm apartment on the UPenn campus in Philadelphia, a fair driving distance from the Bronx where I lived at the time while commuting to NYU. We started calling each other every few days, but with the final rush of papers, exams, and graduation, it was Memorial Day weekend before we went on our first "official" date, a day at the beach in Belmar, on the Jersey shore. Hannah loved the beach, and although I hated baking in the sun, I was happy for any opportunity to see her. We went several times that summer to different beaches in New Jersey and out on Long Island.

Hannah, her parents, and Zelda lived in Maplewood, a popular New York City bedroom community, although not one I'd previously heard of, and I would pick her up with my father's car and drive her back at the end of the day.

Hannah and I went to the movies in Maplewood a few times, and also ventured to the city for dinner or jazz at places in the Village I was familiar with. Whenever we did, we took long walks circling Washington Square Park.

During our walks Hannah would talk animatedly about various books she'd read, was reading, or planned to read, and on occasion she implored me to read some of them. I tried to get through as many as I could that summer, and ended up spending most of the time I wasn't with Hannah reading the books she'd recommended so we could discuss them together.

Hannah's range was impressive. She shifted easily from classics of English, American, and world literature, to Hemingway and other authors of the twentieth century, even to poetry. As an only child, books had been a source of exploration, adventure, even companionship growing up, Hannah told me.

Hannah hoped to inspire other young people to enjoy books as much as she did, and was planning to teach literature at the high school level. Her Teachers College program, a mixture of coursework in the first year followed by a student teaching placement in the second, was "perfect" for what she wanted to do, Hannah said.

I wasn't so much into novels, and tried to interest Hannah in some of the historical works I was more used to reading, but she wasn't very receptive. She said she hadn't taken to history as much as literature. I suggested that might be because many professors teach the subject largely as a dull progression of dates and events without connecting historical eras to those preceding and following them and, ultimately, to modern times. "History is one giant story," I said, trying to relate it to the study of literature.

Hannah was more interested in the "stories within history," like Zelda's, she replied, so I suggested we read some historical fiction. After tossing about a few ideas we settled on *Sophie's Choice*, William Styron's then just recently published novel about the Holocaust, and spent the better part of a mostly overcast day at Belmar discussing it. We'd later go to see the movie version when it was released in December, comparing it to the novel over a few beers at The West End, a bar on Broadway popular with Columbia students.

When talking about her favorite books, Hannah could appear almost manic. But I found her passion for literature stimulating, seductive even. At the end of those long beach days, discussing characters and arguing over convoluted plots, we'd kiss with an ardor matched only by the torrid heat, then calmly plan our next outing. After dropping off Hannah, I would drive home from Maplewood and not remember how I'd gotten back.

We were excited about Columbia and talked about that, as well, where we'd live, the courses we'd be taking, what a future of teaching and research would be like. Hannah was moving into graduate student housing near Teachers College, just north of the main campus. After several visits surveying the bulletin boards, I came across Dick Gorman's flyer in Butler Library, advertising a "single room with bath in charming pre-war building, short walk to campus." I liked the idea of not living in a dorm or sharing a room, and at one hundred fifty dollars a month the price was right.

Neither Hannah nor I was very familiar with the Upper West Side, and once classes started in late-August we began exploring it and other parts of the city, often trying out different music venues. Hannah's taste in music was as eclectic as her appetite for literature, and far broader than mine. She was familiar with the current hits, and whenever we were in the car she'd flip the radio dial wildly, mid-song, until she found the one she liked. One Saturday night at midnight—just after telling me how much she'd enjoyed the reggae band we'd gone to hear down in the Village—Hannah dragged me disco dancing till four in the morning at some swanky club on the East Side. Hannah even enjoyed classical music. In late-September, she got us tickets to a Mozart concert at Lincoln Center, and the one thing I remember about it is dozing off in the middle of what she later said was her favorite Mozart piece, the lively serenade, Eine Klein Nachtmusik. I felt guilty because the tickets were expensive and she'd surprised me with them after I told her I enjoyed classical music and suggested we go to a concert together.

I promised Hannah I'd make it up to her someday.

Chapter Nine

Hannah's birthday fell in October, and I planned what I thought would be a special day: a lecture on the Dead Sea Scrolls at the New York Public Library to be given by a visiting curator from the Israel Antiquities Authority, followed by an afternoon visit to the Cloisters. And to cap off the day, a celebratory dinner near Columbia. When I explained the itinerary to Hannah, she first smirked then burst out laughing.

"I've got to tell Jillian about this. She thinks you're the romantic type. Very romantic taking me to a lecture on the freakin' Dead Sea Scrolls for my birthday."

"I thought you'd enjoy it," I said, putting on one of those fake pouting faces. "I really wanted to go to the Dead Sea Scrolls thing, so I guess you could say it kills two birds with one stone." Hannah's eyes were rolling.

At ten in the morning on that Saturday in October, Hannah and I met at the entrance to Columbia at

116th Street and Broadway. We took the subway to Times Square, then walked over to the main library building at Fifth Avenue and 42nd Street. It was a gorgeous fall day, sunny and cool.

To my surprise, Hannah seemed intrigued by my description of the lecture topic. Although observant, up to that point she hadn't expressed much interest in ancient Jewish history or my area of study, early Christianity. Sensing what I thought could be a break in the dam of that resistance, I assumed the role of docent and began explaining what the scrolls were, where they had been found, and their importance to the study of Second Temple Judaism and early Christian history. Before the talk began she was up to speed.

The lecture ended around one. As we filed out of the Library along with the others, Hannah said she'd enjoyed it and suggested lunch in midtown before heading up to the Cloisters for the rest of the afternoon. She had heard about the Cloisters, as had I, but neither of us had ever been there.

We gulped down a couple of slices at a pizzeria just off of Fifth—Hannah's favorite kosher pizza place, a few blocks away near Rockefeller Center, was closed for the Sabbath—then headed over to Madison to catch the bus up to "Fort Tyron Park—The Cloisters." Fort Tyron Park is in northern Manhattan, past Washington Heights and the George Washington

Bridge. It's also the highest point in Manhattan with a commanding view of the Hudson River.

After we arrived, Hannah led us with an almost childlike exuberance to the Hall of Unicorns, where the tapestries depict the hunt for the mystical Unicorn, an allegory of the passion of Christ, then on to the Gothic Chapel, where the mid-afternoon sunlight danced through the fourteenth-century multi-colored stained glass.

In an odd reversal of roles from the morning visit to learn about ancient scrolls so important to Judaism, Hannah became my guide to the wonders of medieval Christianity. We ended up in the Fuentiduena Chapel, staring at the giant suspended crucifix that is its central focus. Hannah asked jokingly if any of the ones I used to make as a boy on Good Friday afternoons had ever been as large.

Hannah led us next to the Cuxa Cloister, the medieval garden courtyard filled with plants, herbs, and lavender from Provence. The garden is surrounded by an arched walkway hemmed in by columns with ornate Romanesque capitals constructed of Languedoc marble. We circled three or four times before sitting down to rest, our legs dangling over the edge of the base supporting the columns.

"Thank you for taking me here," Hannah said, kissing me on both cheeks, "*faire la bise*," in the French style she explained.

"I should thank you. How do you know so much about this place. I thought you'd never been here?"

"I haven't," Hannah replied. "But a professor who taught this French medieval literature course I took a few years ago told us about it and I've wanted to come ever since."

As we sat together, my hands in my jacket pockets, Hannah put her arms through mine and snuggled close to me, her head resting against my shoulder. She started describing the course and the tradition of courtly love that began with the French troubadours. She talked about some poet I'd never heard of, Chretien de Troyes, and about the Song of Roland. She asked if I minded her going on so much about books, and I told her no, it was one of the things I loved most about her. Talking about books was Hannah's way of opening herself up to and sharing her thoughts and feelings with me. I could listen for hours, I said.

The Song of Roland was a complex tale with many characters, Hannah told me, but she'd been intrigued by one in particular, a strong-willed Saracen woman named Bramimonde. After Charlemagne defeats the Saracens he grants them the choice to convert to Christianity or be killed, but brings Bramimonde to

Aix-la-Chapelle in an effort to win her conversion through love. Bramimonde is finally converted and changes her name to Julienne. But soon afterward she becomes subservient to Charlemagne and the Christian religion.

"Is there some lesson you've drawn from this story?" I asked, with a half-skeptical tone that also betrayed my lack of familiarity with the subject.

"Women must never allow themselves to be controlled by men," Hannah answered, her voice forceful and earnest.

"I'll consider myself warned. Does this apply to all men?" I asked.

"All men," Hannah replied.

~~~

After leaving the museum, Hannah and I walked over to Fort Tyron Park to catch the A train. Stopping to appreciate the views from the Heights and leaning against one of the stone walls that lined the path, Hannah began telling me about Zelda, whose medical and mental condition had deteriorated over the past year, making it difficult for her to be cared for properly at home. Hannah's being away at school again placed even more of a burden on her parents, and her father had broached the subject of placing Zelda in a nursing home. Hannah's mother was very much opposed to the idea, however, and she and Hannah's father had had a nasty argument.

Her parents' argument had upset Hannah, and she started to cry telling me about it. "She's been through so much, first in Germany, then raising my mom all by herself, then the fire that destroyed the hat shop. She really loved that place. It reminded her of her father, and of growing up in Germany before everything fell apart."

I found Hannah's love for her grandmother deeply moving and placed my arm around her shoulders, offering to help in any way I could. In describing how Zelda might feel abandoned in a nursing home, Hannah, usually so vibrant and self-assured, seemed sad and even vulnerable in a way I'd not witnessed before. She turned, looked into my eyes, then embraced me, burrowing her head against my chest and resting it gingerly beneath my chin, as if seeking protection from the chilly, late-afternoon wind suddenly sweeping across the Heights. I had never felt closer to Hannah than in that moment.

I asked Hannah if she wanted to sit down on one of the park benches and stay a bit longer, but she preferred to leave, she said, as it would be getting dark soon. We caught the A train, switched subway lines at 168th Street, then got off at the 116th Street station where we had met up earlier that morning. We decided to walk the remaining ten blocks to my apartment.

As we passed Havana Heaven, a small Cuban restaurant that Hannah and I had gone to before and enjoyed, I suggested we have dinner there to celebrate her birthday. Hannah agreed, but she was tired and wanted to rest a bit before going out again. It had been a long day.

The apartment was dark and cold when we arrived; the heat wouldn't kick in for another few hours. I flipped the light switch near the door and called out to see if either Dick or Iris was home. There was no response. The Gormans had likely gone upstate to their country house, and were no doubt enjoying the fall foliage and a warm fire. I excused myself for a moment to go to my room and returned a few minutes later.

Hannah said she was hungry and wanted a snack before dinner, so we headed into the kitchen. As you entered, there was a battered refrigerator on the right and an old, chipped porcelain gas stove on the left. At the opposite end of the room a second curved doorway led to a small dining alcove filled with a round table and two wicker-backed chairs. A few department-store pictures in cheap plastic frames hung haphazardly on the papered walls, and there were two large windows that, from the apartment's eighth floor perch, offered a majestic view of Riverside Drive as it wound its way north, hugging the Hudson.

In the distance, one could see the George
Washington Bridge; the mass of intertwined steel
cables and glistening lights seemed to heave, but
never give way, under the weight of early evening
traffic. It would be dusk soon, that time when people
make their way home, tired yet at last unburdened
from the day's labors, and glide mindlessly into the
night's primal routines.

As I looked out the window, Hannah arranged
jam, a box of Melba toast, and some slightly wrinkled
grapes on the table. A minute or two later, the kettle
began hissing softly, signaling that tea would be ready
soon.

"I was starving, hope you don't mind," Hannah
said in between crunches.

"No, no, that's fine," I replied, staring at Hannah
as the final rays of the sun streamed through the
alcove window. Her cheeks were rosy red, as were my
own, from the brisk walk down Broadway.

The crunching stopped. "What are you staring
at?" Hannah asked, coyly, the way women do when
they very well know the answer to that question.

"Oh, nothing," I replied, careful not to reveal my
thoughts, before adding in quick succession, "I love
the view from here, when the sun sets over the river
and the bridge." I was certain Hannah saw through
the innocent fib. I'd been gazing dreamily at her curls,

imagining what it would be like to run my fingers through them as we made love for the very first time.

It was a cool evening; the temperature had dropped to the low fifties. Being an inch or two from the window I could sense the chill of the glass. I pressed my hand against the pane; its heat formed a moist relief of my fingers and palm. Neither Hannah nor I spoke, the only sound was the simmering kettle and the occasional crunch of Melba toast. Soon the kettle began screeching and Hannah went to retrieve it. She poured the bubbling water into two cups.

"Michael?" Hannah said. I closed my eyes, imagining Hannah's curls again, and opened them as I turned toward her, awaiting her words with excitement. "There are no lemons?" she blurted out. I sighed, then began quickly rummaging through the refrigerator for some of that flavored lemon juice, the kind that comes in those little plastic bottles shaped like a lemon. I found one.

"Will this do?" I asked.

"It'll have to," Hannah answered with a smirk.

She poured a drop of the lemon juice, took a sip, then poured another. Two teaspoons of sugar went into the mix. I added a few drops and three spoonfuls of sugar to my own cup, and blew into it before putting it down without drinking. I moved around the right side of the kitchen table, turning the light off so we could better appreciate the intensity of the sunset, then walked to the window.

After a few more sips, Hannah walked over to the window where I was, and stood beside me to my left. I glanced downward, without looking directly at her. She was close enough to me that her right hand and my left met ever so slightly. The sensation of her skin against mine, soft and moist to the touch, set my heart racing. I hoped that only I could hear it thumping.

Staring out of the window in silence, Hannah seemed contemplative and suddenly distant. I asked if anything was wrong.

"No," she insisted, turning to me and placing both hands on my chest. "I was only thinking about my grandmother. She's always telling me all she wants is to see me happy, and now she seems to be slipping away, a little more each day, just when . . ." Hannah averted her eyes, her soft voice evincing a kindness of heart, a tenderness of emotion I found myself drawn to ever more irresistibly.

"Anyway," Hannah said a moment later in her typical manner, her voice stronger as she changed the subject from Zelda's sad circumstance. "Thank you for listening to me today. Tell me, what do you think the chances were we would meet up again, at a model UN conference I almost didn't go to, eight years after we moved from the Bronx? I knew there was a reason I said hello to you that Good Friday. Could it be coincidence? My mom told me it must be fate. She says there's a Yiddish phrase, *beshert*, something is 'meant to be.'"

"Yiddish or English, I'm glad you did, because I never would have mustered the courage to say hello to you."

"You may have been shy, but I certainly wasn't," Hannah said boastingly.

"By the way, I have your birthday gift," I said, rather spontaneously, as if some mysterious force had made me think of it.

"What is it? Did you get me one of those scrolls?"

"Well, not quite, but close enough." I opened my hand to reveal a necklace with an intertwined Star of David and heart pendant, which I'd retrieved from my room earlier and put in my shirt pocket. I had meant to present it to Hannah at dinner, but decided on the spur of the moment to give it to her then and there. I placed the necklace around her neck and tightened the clasp.

"It's you and me," I explained. "You've wrapped yourself around my heart, blocking any escape."

"Now you decide to be romantic?" Hannah said in a whimsically sardonic tone. "You're trying to make up for taking me to a lecture about a bunch of dead scrolls on my birthday, aren't you?" I raised my eyebrows and smiled.

"No, really, Michael, it's beautiful. And I love what it says about us."

I took Hannah's hands in mine, but let go as she leaned back into my arms and rested her head gently on my chest, an eruption of light from the setting sun piercing the alcove's darkness and pouring radiantly across her face. I swallowed the honey scent of her hair, and smothered myself in her curls. Remembering how I had meekly sought permission to kiss Hannah that night in Princeton six months before, I now gripped her arms and legs firmly, feeling the contours and rhythms of her body and sensing that, on this night, each of us desired the other unreservedly. Hannah turned and closed her eyes, her breasts pressing against me and her lips, pulsing and full, opening to meet my own. We kissed. Then, just as the sun melted into the river and yielded to the exploding, orange and violet-soaked sky, we surrendered ourselves to each other for what seemed like forever.

Chapter Ten

A few weeks later, Hannah's parents invited me to Shabbos dinner on that Friday of the long Thanksgiving weekend. I asked Hannah what I could bring, and she suggested a particular kosher wine her father enjoyed. After arriving and presenting the wine to him, Hannah's father, Alan, and I chatted for a bit while Hannah helped her mother in the kitchen. Alan was a short, stocky man with jet black hair, combed neatly and parted on the left, and he wore browline glasses, the kind that were popular back in the 1960s. I had met him only twice before, each time briefly, when dropping Hannah off after a night out in the city.

Alan asked whether I'd encountered any traffic on the ride down from the Bronx, telling me how he'd grown up in the borough's Morrisania section and tracing his own family back to the heavy wave of German, including German-Jewish immigration to the Bronx in the mid-nineteenth century, following the failed revolutions of 1848.

Alan said he understood Hannah and I had met at a Model UN conference, at which the NYU team represented Lebanon. He abruptly asked what I thought of "the situation" in Lebanon, and whether Israel had had "any real choice" but to invade the country given the presence of "so many PLO terrorists."

Hannah had told me that her father had a serious interest in Middle East affairs and was likely to bring up the subject, so I wasn't surprised when he dived right into a discussion of the conflict. But I was taken aback—embarrassed would be more accurate—at Alan's apparent presumption I had done extensive research on Lebanon's civil war and complicated political situation in preparation for the Model UN event. In fact, we hadn't gotten final approval from the dean's office, or our country assignment from the organizers until a few days before the start of the conference. And although the subject of many of the courses I'd taken for my history major was the Middle East, and I considered myself knowledgeable about the Arab-Israeli conflict, our team's "research" on Lebanon consisted of a quick dash to the country's consulate where we picked up a handful of position papers that Vania and Gary read aloud on the car ride down to Princeton.

Hannah must have been listening from the kitchen, the next room over from the living room where Alan and I were seated, because when she entered she gently asked him not to "badger" me like he did his friends, and "reminded" him I was pursuing a doctorate in early Christian history not Middle East politics.

"The Maronite Catholics are one of the three powerful groups in Lebanon," Alan replied. "As a student of the Middle East, I'm sure Michael has opinions about what's going on there. I'm interested in hearing them even if you aren't."

"Yes, I am, Dad, but not now; we're just about to eat," Hannah said. Alan rose from his chair in mock submission and said something about how Hannah "always gets her way" before loudly beckoning me to join him. "To be continued," he thundered, dramatically but lightheartedly, placing his left hand on my shoulder and thrusting his finger up in the air as the three of us walked together toward the dining room.

Hannah had told me what to expect during Shabbos dinner—my first—and to follow her lead during the meal. I placed several dollar bills into the tzedakah box on the table. Alan told me that the word "tzedakah" means charity, but explained that it is derived from the root word, "tzedek," meaning justice. "Justice, justice, thou shalt pursue," he intoned, referring me to the oft-quoted proverb found in the Book of Deuteronomy.

I stood along with everyone else as Ruth and Hannah lit the Sabbath candles and the family sang Shalom Aleichem. Alan recited kiddush over the wine—his Hebrew was mellifluous although I had no way to gauge its accuracy—and after the prayers we ate freshly-baked challah bread, then soup, roast chicken with vegetables and potatoes, and a delicious kugel. Hannah jokingly whispered "faux pas" in my ear after I respectfully declined the gefilte fish. The dinner was otherwise largely the Thanksgiving Day meal I'd eaten the day before with my own family.

Ruth started off our dinner conversation with small talk, a good deal of it concerning Melanie, Ruth's assistant at the Manhattan law firm where she was head librarian. Something about Melanie having a bit of an attitude because she was earning an MLS degree, an academic credential Ruth herself did not possess.

Hannah was seated to my right across from Alan, who sat at the head of the table. She was wearing the necklace I'd given her draped over a dark maroon turtleneck sweater. I was excited Hannah had chosen to wear the necklace to dinner, even more when she squeezed my hand under the table after Alan mentioned he had noticed it, just before he shifted the conversation to recent events in the news.

I was trying to convey interest in Alan's mostly political commentaries, but found myself distracted by thoughts of Hannah and me, and so was startled when he turned and asked what I believed the death of Leonid Brezhnev might portend for America's relationship with the Soviet Union and the fate of millions of Russian Jews hoping to emigrate to the West. Perhaps sensing my discomfiture, Ruth interceded, explaining why in her view not much was likely to change on either subject in the near term. I quickly mumbled my agreement, simultaneously squeezing Hannah's left knee and eliciting a discretely repressed smile from her.

After dinner, I joined Alan and Zelda in the living room, while Hannah and Ruth cleared the table and disappeared into the kitchen. As he'd promised, Alan promptly picked up where he had left off earlier in the evening, raising President Reagan's criticism of Israel over the Sabra and Shatila massacres carried out by Israel's Phalangist allies, which had taken place in September only a few months before. He seemed particularly incensed that, back in August, President Reagan had labeled Israel's bombing of Beirut a "holocaust."

"Lebanese Christians butchered those people, yet Israel was blamed. Why do you think that is?" Alan asked after a lengthy monologue.

I knew he wanted me to say the reason was antisemitism and media bias—he had made specific reference to John Chancellor's "biased commentary" on the NBC Nightly News—but I didn't agree. Having read accounts of the massacres in The New York Times and Time Magazine, I believed Israel shared responsibility for them. But, I said I didn't know.

Feeling I needed to respond to Alan in some way, I offered the observation that I didn't think "all the killing" would end until the "fundamental issue" had been resolved, then immediately regretted having done so. Not surprisingly, Alan asked me what that issue was, and I replied, with some trepidation, "justice for the Palestinian people," my reference to justice accurately reflecting my views and, frankly, coming to mind as a result of Alan's earlier evocation of Deuteronomy. It was, nevertheless, a halting, stilted response that betrayed my nervousness, and came off sounding as if I was posing a question to Alan rather than answering his.

"There has never been a *Palestinian people*, Michael. You don't know your history, son," Alan snapped back, dismissively. I wasn't sure if Alan was angry at me for expressing my opinion so directly, or just being forcefully direct with his own, but decided at that point the wiser course was to deflect. I acknowledged, sheepishly, that "there's a lot of history over there and I certainly don't claim to know all of it."

"Alan, please," Ruth seemed to implore as she emerged from the kitchen carrying a tray filled with coffee cups and entered the living room accompanied by Hannah. "Leave the boy alone," she continued. "Don't you know Michael used to live on Willow Tree Lane when we were there? Let's not grill him tonight. He's our guest and Hannah's friend." "Grilling, who's grilling. This isn't a barbecue. I'm just trying to have a conversation." Even I couldn't help but laugh out loud at Alan's attempt to break the tension with humor.

Zelda suddenly spoke up. She hardly had said a word during dinner and had been sitting silently next to Alan in one of the twin armchairs positioned across from the sofa, where Ruth, Hannah and I were seated, a small lamp table between her and Alan. Looking at me and Hannah, she said, in an accented, phlegmatic voice, "I remember you Michael. Hannah told me about your mother. I was sorry to hear. I remember her very well. She bought her house dresses from me. She didn't like Sellinger's; she said his prices were too high. She talked about Italy and the war, about having to beg for crumbs of bread. Those years brought so much suffering." As she finished speaking, Zelda was already winded, her voice fragmenting as she gasped for air and her gaze now fixed somewhere beyond my and Hannah's reach. "So much suffering, so much suffering" she repeated slowly, the words trailing off into silence in an almost otherworldly decrescendo, as if each successive one carried a swelling burden of memory too heavy to bear.

Clasping my hands together, I reacted by leaning toward Zelda and replying, excitedly, "Yes, I remember you, too. We used to visit your shop to buy Easter hats for my sisters." It was the first time I had ever really spoken to Zelda and, knowing how much Hannah loved her, I was anxious to engage her in conversation. I turned momentarily to Hannah. She offered me wide, encouraging eyes. But Zelda said nothing more and only continued to stare and repeat in a breathless monotone that she remembered my mother from Pelham Bay, her own labored eyes conveying some sorrow I could not penetrate, a distance measured in time and pain that seemed incapable of being traversed.

"Mutti, don't tire yourself anymore now, please," Ruth said as she got up from the far end of the sofa where she had been sitting and walked toward Zelda with a pillow in her hand.

"Zelda is right," Alan observed, looking at Hannah and me and a moment after Ruth finished positioning the extra pillow behind Zelda's back. "Those were terrible years. We're all still living in the shadow of the war and the Holocaust. And we will be for generations. We can never let it happen again."

In the lingering, awkward seconds that ensued, Hannah rose to comfort Zelda and handed her a glass of ice water from the table, while I turned to Ruth in an almost desperate effort to avoid engaging Alan further about the conflict. I liked Ruth. I had met her a number of times before that night, once the day Hannah and I first went to the beach at Belmar, on several other occasions in July and August when we'd gone to dinner and a movie in Maplewood, and then again when I helped Hannah move her things into the residence hall at Columbia. Ruth had always been kind to me, and appeared to have a genuine maternal instinct about her. I almost felt she'd been doting on me over the course of the evening, which I appreciated given how bad things seemed to be going with Alan. Ruth gave me the impression she thought I might be a good match for Hannah, or at least I liked to think so.

"Hannah told me about your trip to Israel over the winter break," I said finally, turning my body toward and speaking directly to Ruth.

"Yes, we're all so looking forward to it, especially Hannah," Ruth replied. "Alan spent a few summers there on a kibbutz back in the fifties, and Zelda wants to visit before . . . Well, before it gets too difficult for her to get around."

For a second, I thought it odd of Ruth to refer to her mother by her first name, but then quickly shrugged it off since I'd heard Hannah lightheartedly use "Ruth" when speaking directly to her, even though she always referred to her as "my mom" when talking about her to me. And on other occasions that evening, including a few minutes earlier, I'd heard Ruth call Zelda "mutti," which means "mom" in German.

"Hannah says you decided to go only a few weeks ago."

"Yes," Ruth said. "Hannah's father came up with the idea last month. He just said one day after Hannah's birthday that the family's never been to Israel together and it was about time, so he planned everything within a week, flights, tours, and all."

"Well, the trip sounds wonderful," I said. "I wish I were going."

"Of course," Alan now interjected, "any serious student of Christianity—that's what Hannah tells me you are—must visit Israel, study Judaism, even learn Hebrew. No true Christian can ever hope to fully understand Christianity without a deep knowledge of Judaism and Jewish history."

"Dad, stop!" Hannah implored. From the corner of my eye I could see Ruth glowering at Alan.

"What, am I wrong?" Alan replied, shrugging his shoulders in Hannah and Ruth's direction and presenting them with a feigned expression of indignation. Turning to me with his palms raised upward, he asked, plaintively, "Michael, you're the expert here, am I wrong?"

Maplewood was a bit more than an hour's drive from the Bronx, where I was spending the weekend. I explained that I no longer considered myself a practicing Catholic. But that only elicited a series of questions about when I'd stopped attending Mass and whether I'd "given up" my faith, followed by a short discourse on the Jewish origins of the earliest Christian community. Hannah attempted to change the subject of the conversation, and to draw Ruth and Zelda into it, but her effort fell flat. Alan spoke over her and continued his dialogue with me. I agreed with Alan about the need for students of Christianity—and all Christians—to be knowledgeable about Judaism and Jewish history, then used the excuse of the drive home to say I had to be going.

Alan seemed perturbed at the announcement of my early departure, even asking: "Do you really need to leave so soon?" Before I could answer Ruth and Hannah stood up. Ruth started to thank me for coming and Hannah offered to get my coat. After a round of pleasantries, I expressed my appreciation to Ruth and Zelda for a "lovely meal" and to Alan for "a very stimulating discussion," which, I said, thrusting my finger in the air and imitating his own gesture earlier that evening, was "to be continued." Alan chuckled and slapped my back heartily, replying that he'd be "looking forward to it." Hannah walked with me out to the beat-up Skylark parked in the driveway.

~~~

"Jesus Christ, what was that all about?" I asked Hannah as soon as we were outside and safely beyond earshot of Ruth and Alan.

"I know, my father laid it on pretty thick with the Hebrew prayers. He never does all that for our regular Shabbos dinner," Hannah said, trying to divert attention from what I was sure she knew was my real point.

"No, I wasn't referring to that. I don't think your father likes me very much." It was a statement but also a question.

"I'm not too happy with my dad right now, but please don't be upset," Hannah replied. "My father's an economist, with a PhD from the University of Chicago. In his mind no one is smarter than University of Chicago economists. And like I told you, he's an ardent Zionist and expects everyone to agree with him about Israel, whether or not you're Jewish. It did get a bit heated, but mom and I came to your rescue. You're also the first *goy* I've ever brought home for Shabbos, and my dad's a little bit of the 'date 'em and you'll mate 'em' type. So, there's that, too."

"I guess I should relish the thought of being your first test case."

To be honest, I couldn't detect any difference between Alan's "date and mate" sentiment and similar comments I'd heard from members of my family. I had been told Hannah was "a very smart and pretty girl," just before being asked, "Aren't there any smart and pretty Italian girls at Columbia?" And my pesky Aunt Rita, undoubtedly acting as family emissary, had dutifully pointed out to me that "If you marry a Jewish girl, your kids are gonna be Jewish. You know that, right?" I was, frankly, more upset at Alan's pointed remark about my lack of knowledge regarding the history of the conflict.

"Stop worrying," Hannah reassured me. "My mom adores you, and she's working on my dad. She thinks you have a gentle soul, even if it's a gentile one." I smiled, Hannah's remark easing my concerns temporarily.

I began pouting in a silly, little boy's voice about Hannah's leaving me. "What am I supposed to do while you're in Israel for two weeks?"

"Spend time with your family?" Hannah suggested, innocently enough.

"Should I repeat the question?" I said, my own feelings far less so.

"Work on your Greek, then," Hannah proposed. I was struggling with my New Testament Greek course and barely going to eke out a B, so it made sense to devote time to preparing for the second semester, which was almost certainly going to be tougher than the first.

But I was less than thrilled by the prospect of spending a month drilling down on Greek declensions, and asked Hannah if she could recommend a novel to read during the cold, lonely weeks she'd be away in Israel. After being with Hannah for six months, I'd begun to enjoy fiction far more than I had in the past.

"Give me a suggestion, something I can use to escape from my family while you're off discovering your heritage."

Hannah turned her head upward for a moment, twitching her nose a bit like Elizabeth Montgomery used to do in *Bewitched*. "I have it," she said. "*The Magus*, by John Fowles. It's a great book, long, complicated, and a fantastic plot. It'll keep you thinking for a while, at least until I get back and we can figure it out together. Wait here, I'll get you my copy. It's upstairs."

Hannah's well-worn paperback copy of *The Magus* in hand, I kissed her goodnight and thanked her again for "rescuing" me. I spent the car ride agitated about Alan's barb that I didn't know my history. I promised myself I'd be better armed the next time.

Chapter Eleven

Hannah and her family left for Israel the day after Christmas, and returned two weeks later. She called after getting home and we talked for hours about the trip. They had spent several days in Jerusalem, visiting the Western Wall, the Knesset, Yad Vashem, and Theodore Herzl's grave, among other sites, then Lake Kinneret, the Dead Sea, and Masada, even traveling down to Eilat for an overnight trip before heading back up to Tel Aviv for the return flight home. Ruth stayed behind with Zelda the day Hannah, her father, and the tour group visited Masada, since it would have been too much of a strain for her. I was green with envy, as I longed to see all the places Hannah had visited, and even more to see them together with her.

"You're not thinking of making aliyah?" I asked only half-jokingly, for a brief moment concerned that Hannah's enthusiastic description suggested otherwise.

"No," Hannah assured me. "But I *definitely* want to go back there. I know you'd find it fascinating. We're going together, I promise. You can do field work."

"I'm going to hold you to that promise. I'd love nothing more than to visit Israel with you," I replied.

~~~

Hannah returned to campus a few days before classes resumed. Given our conflicting schedules we saw each other only two or three times during the week, typically for a quick lunch, but then spent weekends together. We would pass lazy Saturday afternoons reading in Butler Library, followed by late-afternoon strolls down Broadway and early-evening dinners at places that struck our fancy and we could afford. Eventually, we'd meander back to the apartment for long nights of watching, and debating, classic old movies we rented for the VCR, and making love while listening to cassette tapes of Iris' violin sonatas and Dick's vintage collection of Edith Piaf records. On Sunday mornings, we would bundle up and race over to Dimitri's for crispy French toast laced with cinnamon and steaming hot oatmeal smothered in brown sugar.

Hannah usually planned outings for us on Sundays to museums or Central Park, or to other parts of the city. One frozen Sunday in February, the day before Valentine's Day, she suggested we venture up to the Bronx Zoo. But we didn't last long there, opting for the indoor exhibits mostly. Afterward, we took the subway back to Columbia and walked over to Riverside Park to kill some time before a Valentine's dinner at Piccolo Paese, a hole-in-the-wall Italian restaurant I'd discovered on Amsterdam Avenue that had homemade pasta and a handful of little round tables covered with old-fashioned plaid tablecloths.

It had taken more than a month because of its length and my coursework commitments, but I'd finally finished reading *The Magus* and was anxious to ask Hannah about it. She'd been right about the book. I'd found it to be a real page-turner. It's the story of Nicholas Urfe, a young Oxford graduate who takes a job teaching English on a remote Greek island called Phraxos. After a time Urfe gets bored and begins exploring another part of the island. He stumbles upon an old estate and meets its mysterious owner, Maurice Conchis—the magus, or sorcerer.

Urfe is drawn into a series of psychological games involving Conchis and a beautiful woman named Lily, who Urfe falls madly in love with and feels he must possess. As the novel progresses, Conchis' manipulation of Urfe intensifies and Lily is transformed into two other characters, Julie and Vanessa. The denouement is a bizarre fantasy scene where Urfe is tormented by a large cast of characters, some known, some unknown, only for the entire episode to be revealed as an elaborate social experiment designed by Conchis to test the limits of Urfe's endurance and capacity to bear humiliation. Urfe returns to England, and, after more mysteries about Conchis are revealed, but left unexplained, he tries and fails to rekindle his relationship with his former lover, Alison. But the book ends inconclusively.

"I could never tell the difference between reality and illusion. And at first I thought Nicholas and Alison would get back together, and I wanted them to, but they never did. I don't know why. I didn't understand the ending at all."

"You weren't supposed to," Hannah replied. In the professorial tone she sometimes used when talking to me about her favorite books, she proceeded to retell various points in the plot, explaining some, leaving the meaning of others dangling for me to attempt to grasp.

"The text keeps you thinking, as you search for different meanings. The search *becomes* the meaning."

"Right," I said, slow-rolling the letter "r" in order to sound skeptical. "And the ending? Even you can't explain it."

"It's subject to different interpretations so the reader is left to decide. It's a literary device known as indeterminacy."

"Well, whatever you call it, the ending was unsatisfying," I grumbled. "After such a wild story I craved finality. I needed to understand it all."

"Life isn't like that. And books reflect life, so why should they be any different?"

It was now late-afternoon and getting dark. I felt the scent of impending snow in my nose, the kind you smell when the cold air and humidity trigger a reaction in your brain. Hannah was wearing a tight-fitting black winter jacket with one of those fur-edged hoods, and it crafted an enticing portrait of her face. Walking in the fading light, we found ourselves in a strangely isolated spot under a canopy of trees stripped bare by winter. We were holding hands, but I felt her fingers slowly slip through mine, and she walked ahead alone as if perceiving something ethereal in the cluster of twisted branches. I came up behind her, gently took her arms and spun her around to me, then kissed her.

"Hey, you like to steal kisses," Hannah said.

"You stole a kiss nine years ago, remember? That's what started it."

I took a step closer. "And what about my heart? I let you steal that without complaining about it."

"Never give all the heart!" Hannah shouted at me.

"What's that supposed to mean?" I said, startled at her reaction.

"It's Yeats' poem. He wrote it about Maud Gonne, an Irish nationalist who broke his heart. Yeats asked her to marry him four times, but she turned him down each time. She married another Irish nationalist."

"Maybe Yeats should have gotten the message sooner. He doesn't seem to have realized what he was up against."

"We might not have a lot of his poems. She was his muse."

"And what about your heart?" I asked. "It is Valentine's."

"My heart is my business. I'm just telling you what Yeats said so you can protect your own."

"Quite the weisenheimer today!"

I moved closer and, slipping my fingers inside Hannah's hood and cupping her face with my hands, kissed her once on each cheek, invitingly.

"*Faire la bise*," I said in my best, improvised French accent.

"Dick and Iris?" Hannah whispered in reply, her lips so close to mine her breath mingled with my own, forming a cloud in the bitterly cold air.

"Upstate till the morning," I answered.

"It's a lot warmer in the monk's cell," Hannah said, using the phrase she'd coined for my room. She called the Gormans' apartment the "monastery" because Iris was never with Dick during the week, and he and

I often ate dinner together in silence before retiring to our rooms for the night.

Entranced by Hannah's gaze, and holding her in my arms, we kissed just as the first swirl of snowflakes began falling furiously around us. I sensed Hannah's desire, as well as my own, and we started back to the apartment. As between us, the boundary separating passions of the intellect from those of the senses was ill-defined and transitory, and in those last, now dreamlike weeks of winter we crossed over it and back with abandon.

Chapter Twelve

As the hardened earth of winter gave way to the budding new life of spring, Zelda took a sharp turn for the worse. She was in and out of the hospital several times in March and April, and on three occasions I picked up the car in the Bronx and drove Hannah from Manhattan to Maplewood so she could visit with her. The family was being told there was little more that could be done and that Zelda's rapidly failing heart left her susceptible to debilitating, maybe even deadly strokes. I tried my best to distract Hannah during those stressful weeks, and for the one-year anniversary of our meeting at Princeton planned a special Saturday night dinner in the city.

I'd read a review in The New York Times of a restaurant at 65th and Third Avenue called The Sign of the Dove, and went there one afternoon to check it out. The tables were spaced far apart, and the three sections of the dining area were separated by two red-brick walls, with three arched openings allowing diners in each section to see the other diners while still maintaining a sense of intimacy. It was kitschy but seemed perfect for my purpose, which was not only to celebrate the anniversary but also to give Hannah a novelty music box I'd come across in the Village. I was sure she'd like it because of her love for Mozart, and I wanted to make up for dozing off at Lincoln Center months before, as I promised Hannah I would. I booked the reservation once I realized the walled arches reminded me of the arched courtyard of the Cuxa Cloister.

~~~

Hannah sounded frantic on the phone. She had just received a call from Ruth who told her Zelda had been taken to the hospital and was in intensive care. It was a mid-week in April, Tuesday or Wednesday I can't recall, and Hannah told me she was leaving to take the train to Maplewood to meet her mother at the hospital. Unless her grandmother's condition deteriorated further, Hannah said, she planned to return on Sunday to finish papers due the following week.

Zelda's condition stabilized, so Hannah decided to return to the city. I met her at Penn Station Sunday morning, and accompanied her to the apartment near Teachers College. I brought us hot tea and lemon. It was a habit I had developed after meeting Hannah. Prior to that, I'd been a three-cup-a-day coffee drinker for years, having been weaned on the strong, Italian-style espresso my mother made each morning and evening.

I didn't disturb Hannah that week so she could focus on her papers. She called me Wednesday to say she was on her way back to New Jersey to spend the rest of the week, and then the weekend, at home. I said I wanted to get together, to give her support and drive her to the hospital if she needed me to. It was an excuse to see and be with her given what she and her parents were going through. I told her I would come by Friday afternoon after picking up my father's car. He'd retired by that point and hardly ever drove the thing anymore. Hannah agreed, and we planned on a light picnic and spending the afternoon in Memorial Park, in Maplewood. I was hoping the day would be a distraction for her.

When I arrived Friday just after noon, Hannah was waiting for me outside, which I didn't recall her ever having done before, and she rushed us into the car. I felt something was amiss, but couldn't tell what might be wrong. I asked Hannah if her mother was at home, since I didn't want Ruth thinking I had been rude by not saying hello or expressing my sympathies about Zelda. Hannah said only that her mother was upset and preparing to go to the hospital.

We drove to the Park, then found a bench in the corner of the picnic area, a fair distance from the screaming toddlers in the nearby playground. Hannah had made us a couple of sandwiches for lunch and I dispatched mine quickly, but she seemed to barely touch hers.

"What's wrong?" I asked. "You haven't said anything since we got here. I thought your grandmother was stable."

"Yes, she's stable for now."

"Is anything else wrong? Are you upset about something?"

Hannah insisted nothing was wrong, but again hardly said a word. I ended up talking in circles with myself.

To this day, I'm still not sure what led me to bring it up at that particular moment, rather than at our Princeton anniversary dinner the next night, as I had intended. I guess I felt a mixture of pride in having a letter to the editor published in The New York Times, and a bit of exasperation at not being able to get through to Hannah about any other subject.

"Hey, did you happen to see my letter in The Times yesterday?" I asked.

"I did," Hannah said, sounding annoyed as she turned and faced me. "And so did my father. That was an enjoyable dinner conversation Michael, thank you very much! You know my father reads The Times, religiously. You could have at least warned me."

I was caught off guard by Hannah's reaction. Had Zelda not been in the hospital and so gravely ill, I almost certainly would have told her the week before about sending in the letter, probably even sought her input before mailing it. But, not wanting to disturb Hannah because of Zelda's condition and the papers she was working on for her classes, I sent it to The Times without telling her.

"I hadn't thought of that. I guess I should have known he might see it, but I never thought they'd publish it. They don't tell you when they decide to publish a letter, so I had no way of knowing. I was surprised as anyone. Why, was he upset about it?"

Hannah pursed her lips, and bobbed her head up and down slightly.

"Just a little," she said in an acerbic tone.

"Did he read the article I responded to? The guy who wrote it is some kind of extremist. He basically said that Israel should have carte blanche in the West Bank and Palestinians no say in their future. That they have no political rights. Forget about Camp David and autonomy, I guess. It was just crazy."

"My father said he's a big name in the New York Jewish community, and a prominent international lawyer to boot. I think he knows a little bit more about the situation than you do. Even the lawyers in my mom's firm must know of him. She's probably embarrassed, too, but would never say anything. Look, it doesn't matter. I don't want to argue about it."

"Well, it sort of does," I replied, feeling combative. Although it was puerile, I had hoped Hannah at least would have complimented me on being published in The New York Times, even if she—or her father— didn't agree with me.

"I didn't think I needed to get your permission to express my opinion about Israel in The New York Times, and I didn't write the letter with the intention of upsetting your father, who I guess agrees with that crackpot."

Hannah looked at me, visibly angry.

"Are you saying my father is a crackpot?"

"No," I insisted. "I'm just saying I have a right to express my opinion about the situation there, and criticize Israel, even if your father disagrees with me."

"Of course you can, Michael. But you can never fully understand my father and other Jews' point of view about it."

"Why?" I asked, in a skeptical tone.

"Because you're not Jewish," Hannah shouted, loud enough that it caused me to turn my head to see if anyone might have overheard.

"You can never understand how Jews have suffered throughout history," she continued. "Everything my family and other Jews went through in Germany, the camps, the killing. The hate my father had to deal with growing up, or how we were made to feel when we lived in Pelham Bay. And you know my grandmother's shop was burned to the ground because she's Jewish. I told you it was arson. You can never know what it's like to be Jewish, or why Israel is so important to us."

I was taken aback by Hannah's retort.

"Are you blaming me for the fire now?" My response was nonsensical, but I was genuinely at a loss as to what to say.

"Of course not, Michael, don't be stupid," Hannah replied, with typical, but on this occasion jarring, bluntness.

"Hannah, I've never given you a reason to believe I don't understand what your grandmother went through in Germany, or what you and your parents went through in Pelham Bay, or the significance of Israel to Jewish people. You know I understand the history and what happened to Jews during the war. In Italy, the Germans murdered my uncle, shot him in cold blood for no reason. My father had to tell my grandmother and take her to the shallow grave where they dumped his body. She collapsed in his arms. I get what happened during the war, I get it."

"You never told me that story, Michael. It's terrible, it really is."

Hannah paused for a moment. "But it's not the same. As bad as what they did to your uncle, it's not the same as hating an entire group of people and planning to kill all of them because of their religion, just because they're Jews."

I told Hannah I didn't think her comment was fair as I had never meant to equate the random killing of civilians by German soldiers with the planned extermination of Jews in the Holocaust. But I hesitated to say anything more. I was confused by Hannah's sudden antagonism, but she was obviously very upset and underlying everything was the fact that her beloved grandmother lay near death in a hospital bed a few miles away. I railed at my insensitivity and petty conceit about the letter, and just wanted to turn back the clock.

"Hannah, I never should have brought up my letter given what you've got going on. Let's take a walk, or talk about something else, please. Or I can take you home, or to the hospital if you want."

"No, it's fine," Hannah said. But I knew she didn't mean it.

I couldn't recall having argued with Hannah like this before, even on those many occasions we'd discussed the conflict. Ironically, it had been my interest in the Holocaust, and discussions with Hannah about its depiction in literature and film, that had led me to delve more deeply into the related subject of the creation of Israel and its impact on the Palestinians. My interest having grown as a result of those conversations, I began attending, occasionally with Hannah, monthly meetings sponsored by a group called Students for Middle East Understanding over at the Union Theological Seminary, which had an affiliation with Columbia.

Although in those days there was a fair amount of discussion on campus about what was then still referred to as the "Arab-Israeli conflict," it wasn't the focus of as much attention, or agitation as, say, the struggle against apartheid in South Africa. Only a week before our visit to Memorial Park, Hannah and I walked past an angry demonstration of students calling for an end to apartheid and chanting, "South Africa must be free. Free Mandela now." We hadn't encountered any similar demonstrations about the Palestinian struggle. But in 1983, both the promise and disappointment of Oslo still lay years ahead in the future, and it would be decades before Israel's treatment of Palestinians would begin to be described as apartheid.

"Maybe it's best if you take me home. I'll go to the hospital later," Hannah said finally. Remembering how distracted and distant Hannah seemed when I picked her up earlier, I couldn't help but wonder if there was something more to it all than my letter to The Times.

"Hannah, I said I was sorry. I didn't mean to upset you or your father, or whoever else I upset. Honestly, when I read the article it reminded me of your father so maybe I wrote the letter as a way of getting back at him, and proving him wrong, because of what he said to me at dinner that night about not knowing the history. I never thought they'd publish it."

"What?" Hannah said, angrily.

"Oh never mind, please. That's such bullshit. Forget I said it. Let's just go. Fuck The Times. Fuck the conflict."

The edges of Hannah's eyes were now filled with tears. She asked me to drive her home and I did. It was the longest seven minutes of my life.

When I returned the car to the Bronx, I learned that shortly after leaving that morning Hannah had called. She'd said that she wasn't feeling up to getting together and hoped to catch me before I left. A few minutes later, I called The Sign of the Dove and canceled our reservation.

Chapter Thirteen

Zelda passed away less than a week after that day in Memorial Park. It was discovered that a number of mini-strokes had landed her in the hospital ICU the week before, and she suffered a major brain hemorrhage the next Monday. She had for the most part lost consciousness as a result of the initial strokes, and died early Wednesday evening without ever regaining it.

The service was held Friday morning. I sat with Jillian and Hannah's other friends behind three rows filled with a number of Ruth's colleagues from the law firm—Ruth had no extended family to speak of—and members of Alan's family. Hannah's eulogy for Zelda, delivered with a "shattered heart" for a "wonderful bubbe" whose "own heart overflowed with kindness, tenderness, and love" was lyrical and moving, and brought tears to many eyes, including my own.

Following the burial, Hannah's friends and I went back to the house for a bit, but I didn't stay long. I drove out to Maplewood again on Sunday, the third night of Shiva. Ruth was gracious and didn't let on that she knew about what had happened between Hannah and me at Memorial Park, although I was certain she did. Afterward, I drove Hannah back to her apartment near Columbia, but she mostly talked about the papers she had to complete and hardly mentioned Zelda.

Over the next few weeks, I called Hannah several times, but she seemed to come up with excuses not to get together. She even stopped asking me to join her for Saturday morning services. Since returning from Israel, she'd been attending one of the nearby synagogues more regularly than she had in the past, and at her invitation I'd been accompanying her.

I knew Hannah would be moving out of the residence hall and back to New Jersey when the semester ended. As that date approached, I'd been pestering her about our getting together before she left for the summer. The night before the last day of exams she called and agreed to meet in front of Butler Library. Under an annoying, on-again, off-again drizzle we walked several times around the Quad, which was filled with tipsy students celebrating the end of the school year. But Hannah declined my suggestion we go somewhere quiet to talk.

"I don't know what's happened with us, Hannah, but I want to make things right," I said. "Why won't you talk to me about what's going on?" I was feeling hurt and confused.

"Michael, I need time alone," Hannah replied after a silent moment. "Away from you, my parents, everyone. Time to process a lot of things that have been going on, things that I've learned."

"What things, Hannah? About me, something you've learned about me? I don't understand this." I hesitated to bring up Memorial Park.

"I'm not sure I understand it, either. Things aren't always capable of being explained or meant to be fully understood."

"Hannah, please don't. This is not a hermeneutics lesson."

Hannah bowed her head, and I could tell she didn't want to talk further. Leaving campus and turning on Broadway, we walked back to the residence hall.

"The last thing I want is to pressure you," I said, backing away as Hannah approached the doorway. "Take the time you need. I'll be here when you're ready to talk. Just please don't make any decisions without me, promise?"

Hannah looked up. "Promise," she replied with sad eyes, before saying she loved me and kissing me goodnight. It was the reassurance of her love that I had been craving.

~~~

For the next two weeks, I found myself in a state of suspended animation of sorts, listless, unable to read, concentrate, or do much of anything but remonstrate myself for every perceived slight against Hannah. Then, at the very end of May, Hannah called and said she was going to Israel, alone. She wasn't sure for how long, maybe a few weeks, maybe for the summer. I was shocked and told her so.

"You promised you wouldn't make any decisions without talking to me. You promised we'd go to Israel together."

"I know, and we will someday. But for now I'm going alone."

"Can I ask why you're going?"

"I need to figure out some things by myself, explore some things about my grandmother. I'll explain it all when I get back."

I didn't understand what was happening—whether the turning point had been Memorial Park or was yet to come—but told Hannah I would be waiting for her when she returned.

Chapter Fourteen

For the summer, I'd landed a job as an editorial assistant at *Columbia*, the university's alumni magazine, which meant I'd essentially be a gopher for the editor-in-chief, Bianca, a rather eccentric and demanding Italian character with a penchant for expensive Mont Blanc fountain pens and magenta-colored ink. Returning from work late one afternoon, almost a week after Hannah left for Israel, Dick told me Ruth had phoned. I called her back as soon as Dick went in for his customary half-hour nap before dinner.

"Thank you for getting back to me so quickly, Michael. I'm worried about Hannah."

"Why, what's happened?" I asked anxiously.

"Well, you know she arrived in Israel last week. She'd been staying in a hostel in Jerusalem, but when I called yesterday they told me she checked out two days ago. We haven't heard from her since. Alan says we need to leave her alone and that when he took his college summer trip to Europe he didn't contact his parents for weeks. But I'm worried and don't know what to do."

"Have you called the embassy or the police in Jerusalem? They'd know if something had happened, wouldn't they?"

"Yes, I've called them both, but they say there's nothing they can do because she's an adult and I have no reason to think anything suspicious has happened, especially since it's only been a few days. The Jerusalem police said they get these calls all the time and it's not unusual for kids to wander around the country, especially in summer, and forget to call their parents."

"Hannah said she needed time alone. I think we have to respect that."

"I know, but I'm just concerned. She hasn't called you, has she?"

I now suspected Ruth's finding out the answer to that question was the reason for her call.

"No, of course not," I answered. "I would have told you if she had."

"Well, I guess there's not much more I can do but wait for her to call me. I'm sorry to have bothered you, Michael. Alan would be livid if he knew I'd called you about this."

I don't know what drove me to say what I said next. Maybe it was a desire to salvage things with Hannah. Maybe I read too much into Ruth's calling, and misinterpreted our conversation as her plea for me to go and meet Hannah in Israel so we could work out together whatever it was that had compelled her to go there. Maybe Hannah wanted me to go, as a test of my love for her, and had put Ruth up to making the call. Ruth didn't say any of those things, at least, as I rationalized it, not in so many words. In retrospect, it was certainly just wishful thinking on my part. But what I told Ruth was I'd be willing to go to Israel to look for Hannah, if only to make sure she was safe. And if she still wanted to be alone, I'd turn right around and take the first plane back.

Ruth's response, "Thank you so much, Michael. You don't know what that means to me," was all I needed to hear.

I promptly took pen to paper. Hannah had taken a backpack planning to travel around the country for an indefinite time, and hadn't made reservations; she had first telephoned Ruth from the student hostel in Jerusalem. I told Ruth I'd update her with my arrangements and call her before I left and again after arriving. I asked her to call me right away if she heard anything from Hannah.

Columbia's bookstore was closed, but as soon as I finished talking to Ruth, I rushed to the Coliseum Bookstore near Lincoln Center and bought one of those guidebooks, *Frommer's Israel On $25 & $30 a Day.* Early the next morning, I was at a travel agency on 96th and Broadway exploring options to get to Israel as soon as I could.

I told my father I had to go to Israel for a few days to fulfill a requirement for my graduate program I'd previously been unaware of, and told Bianca I had to go to Italy to deal with a family emergency. I almost certainly failed to convince my father I was telling the truth about Israel. It was anyone's guess whether I convinced Bianca about my trip to "Italy," but all that mattered was she approved it. She even said she wanted to hear all about the trip when I returned.

The travel agent told me the cheapest way to get to Israel on such short notice was to take a Sunday night charter flight to Rome, which had an available seat due to a couple's last minute cancellation, then connect to an El Al flight to Tel Aviv on Monday. I'd have five days and nights in Israel, and needed nine hundred dollars for the flights. I had to scramble, and quick. Borrowing five hundred dollars each from Pat and my sister, and raiding my own meager bank account—I hadn't yet been paid by the magazine—I put together about fifteen hundred dollars to pay for the flight, and for travel and hotel expenses while in Israel.

Although the flight's departure was delayed, we made up the time en route and landed in Rome on schedule. Occupying the seat next to mine was another backpacker, and we struck up a conversation.

Hailing from Chicago, Dan Weiler had finished a one-year master's program in Middle East studies at the University of Michigan, and had been accepted to its law school for the fall.

As a last fling of sorts with his "true passion" before entering the mundane world of law, Dan planned a three-week jaunt through Israel, with an initial stop in Cairo. Because of the Egypt-Israel peace treaty brokered by President Carter, the border between the two countries was open. Dan planned to spend a couple of days exploring Cairo before taking a bus through the Sinai and up to the Rafah Crossing into Gaza. From there he'd make his way to Tel Aviv, Jerusalem, and wherever else in Israel his wanderlust led him in the time he had. I told him his plan sounded like the adventure of a lifetime. When Dan asked why I was going to Israel I gave him the "doctoral program" version and he appeared to buy it.

Dan talked for most of the nine-hour flight. I laughed endlessly, at times hysterically, at his tales of madcap college exploits and prodigious sexual conquests, most of which seemed unbelievable or at least comically exaggerated. But by the time we disembarked in Rome, I had half a mind to throw caution to the wind, cancel my reservation in Jerusalem, and join him on his escapade. I thought better of the idea only after reminding myself that

I was on my way to Israel as much for Ruth and Hannah's sake as my own. By that point, Dan had set off on a sprint to catch his Egypt Air connection to Cairo. I was sorry to see him go.

El Al security control in Rome was a hiccup I hadn't anticipated. I was a twenty-three-year-old bearded male traveling alone, on a U.S. passport that expired in less than a year. My backpack was picked clean, and I faced a series of probing questions about the purpose for my visit to Israel, where I planned to stay, who I planned to see, and whether I'd been separated from my luggage or been given anything to deliver to someone in Israel. The security officers seemed suspicious at first, but the combination of my Columbia University ID, confirmed reservation at a hotel in Jerusalem, and explanation that amounted to a hybrid of Dan's "last summer fling" and "field research" for doctoral studies in the history of Christianity finally worked.

I faced a similar battery of searches and questions at Ben Gurion Airport. I was asked repeatedly about why I was visiting Israel—a very good question I kept asking myself—but having already been cleared through Rome must have helped. I grabbed my backpack and made a beeline for the taxi stand.

Chapter Fifteen

The first order of business when I got to my hotel was to call Ruth to see if Hannah had contacted her. She still had not, Ruth said, so I went off to find the hostel Hannah had stayed in when she first arrived. As they were wary of my questions about their former guest, the fact I was aware of Ruth's call a few days before was only enough to buy confirmation from the manager that "a Miss Hannah Lindemann" had stayed the prior week but checked out without providing further contact information, which, I was told, was not at all unusual. It was a dead end, the same information Ruth had given me.

I spent my first night marking up the Frommer's guide, along with a *Baedeker's Israel* I'd picked up at JFK, for every hostel and budget hotel listing in Jerusalem. Ruth had said Hannah would be on a shoestring budget, so I felt it safe to assume I wouldn't find her poolside at the King David.

The next day, Tuesday, I visited every place where I thought Hannah might be staying or might have stayed. I also visited the U.S. Consulate and several local police stations to see if any reports had been filed; there were none. Back in my hotel in East Jerusalem that night, I checked off the hotels and hostels I'd been able to visit during the day. And I kept hoping that when I called Ruth later that night she'd say Hannah had gotten in touch with her so she could tell me where Hannah was in Jerusalem, or elsewhere in Israel, and I could find her. But when I spoke to Ruth she had no news.

Having visited nearly all of the hostels and budget hotels I had identified that allowed inquiries about their guests, and unable to resist the many historical temptations of Jerusalem, I decided the next day to explore the Old City.

Starting out in the cool, early morning shade of Gethsemane's olive groves, I contemplated what it must have been like the night Jesus was betrayed and arrested, remembering the apocryphal story we'd been told back at St. Regina about how he had sweated beads of blood as he prayed to be spared the bitter cup that awaited him.

Descending the Mount of Olives and entering the Old City through St. Stephen's Gate, I made my way to the iconic Western Wall, but felt out-of-place in the crowd of mostly Jewish worshippers who filled the plaza in front of it. As I milled about with a sort of aimless awe, an Orthodox man with a heavy beard and sidecurls approached me, asking, "Are you Jewish?" I said no, intending to explain my reasons for being in Jerusalem. But before I could say anything more, the man abruptly turned and walked away without another word.

Exiting the plaza, I ascended the steps leading up to the Haram al-Sharif, where the Second Temple had once stood. In the Dome of the Rock shrine, I gazed upon the great stone platform of Mount Moriah, the spot, Genesis tells us, where God commanded Abraham to sacrifice Issac as a "burnt offering." Ruminating on the ancient scene, I couldn't help but recall Kierkegaard's characterization of religious faith as the "highest passion in a human being." The *Akedah*—the story of the binding of Issac—had been foundational to Judaism and would later serve as the exemplar for the germinal Christian dogma of God's sacrifice of his own, incarnate son, Jesus. That the story was nothing more than an allegorical myth had never diminished its narrative power to captivate those with faith enough to believe it, or, through an accretive process lasting centuries, to sear itself into a people's collective memory and historical consciousness.

Returning to St. Stephen's Gate, I set out upon the Via Dolorossa, following the Stations of the Cross along with a gaggle of Christian tourists. Breaking away from the crowd for a few minutes, I stopped in the Arab Souk to buy a scarf and scented soap in anticipation of seeing Hannah that day, or the next, or the day after that.

The Way of Sorrows ends at the Church of the Holy Sepulchre, built over the traditional site of Jesus' tomb and resurrection, and almost certainly the most sacred Christian site in the world. The Church, with its magnificent dome and inner chapel, isn't dated from Jesus' time, of course; its fame rests instead on the legend of the "true Cross" that only emerged after the Emperor Constantine's mother, Helen, visited Jerusalem as a pilgrim early in the fourth century. The fact is our knowledge of the origins of Christianity is largely textual—the earliest Christians spoke to us through words, not stones—and there's so much we don't know about the critical years between the Crucifixion and the destruction of the Second Temple in 70 C.E., the era that fascinated me the most and a time when, as Alan had taken pains to remind me at dinner, the Followers of the Way were considered members of an insignificant Jewish sect.

Unlike many of the other visitors, who from their conversations appeared vitalized by having had re-enacted Christ's passion to its denouement, I emerged from the Church feeling empty and disheartened, all the more so since I'd gone in with a genuine sense of anticipation, even a lingering reverence of sorts. Given the site's significance, I felt no small amount of guilt, bordering on sinfulness, at having had such a muted reaction.

I had come to Israel to find Hannah, not recover some bygone religiosity, I said in silent self-reproach. And yet, I thought, perhaps it was me who was lost. Had I truly reconciled myself to the abandonment of Catholicism years before, or was I, to some uncertain extent, still captive to the salvific fable of Christianity? Was enrolling at Columbia, I wondered, nothing more than a temporizing means to straddle the chasm that existed between the Jesus of faith, who as a boy drawn to the mysteries of the magisterium I longed to know and love as the Son of God, and the only hardly less mysterious Yeshua of history, who was all that remained for me once I could no longer believe he had been anything other than simply a man?

Without hope of answering those questions, but cognizant of the late hour, I raced by taxi over to West Jerusalem to visit Theodore Herzl's grave before closing time, and ended the brilliantly sunny afternoon strolling the Carob tree-lined Avenue of the Righteous Gentiles leading to Yad Vashem.

The contrast between the Church's ornately orchestrated mysticism and the memorial's austere depiction of the Holocaust's murderous reality could not have been more stark. Surrounded by death at every turn, I stared into the faces of the slaughtered innocents whose photographs lined the ten-meter cone in the Hall of Names, their eyes frozen in time and beseeching me from across the decades. I stood in solemn silence in the Hall of Remembrance, its walls fashioned of rough-hewn basalt boulders drawn from the quarries near Lake Kinneret. Looking down, I read the names of the twenty-two extermination and concentration camps written in white letters on the black floor, and then, along with the others, cast my gaze upward as the smoke emitted by the Eternal Flame wafted its way to the ceiling of the great Hall. The story told at Yad Vashem was no legend.

I had read many books about the Holocaust since watching *QB VII* and choosing the Bantam paperback edition of Lucy Dawidowicz's classic, *The War Against The Jews*, for my first high school book report in European history, the same course at Xavier I would teach years later. And I was trying hard to feel what Hannah and other Jews might feel standing where I was. But I couldn't help wonder if Hannah had been right, that I would never be able to understand the Holocaust in the way she and they did, or feel the enormity of it in the same visceral, personal sense. I thought about how Hannah had promised we would visit Israel together, and how we were both there at the same time yet apart from each other, separated by the gulf between her history and my own. I despaired of our ever being able to bridge the gap again. All I wanted was to find Hannah, to be with her.

I left the memorial feeling the same sadness I had felt those many years before, after speaking with Hannah for the first time that blindingly sunny Good Friday afternoon and then weeks later learning, also for the first time, about the Holocaust—overwhelmed by the sheer, incomprehensible tragedy of it, but, more than anything, missing Hannah.

~~~

Emotionally drained and exhausted from the day's travels, I fell fast asleep before calling Ruth as I'd planned to. I did the next day, waiting until one in the afternoon to take account of the time difference. She told me Hannah had finally called the night before and was safe. I asked anxiously where she was so I could meet her, but Ruth said Hannah hadn't told her where, only that she was safe and that was what was important. I agreed, but knew she was lying. Hannah wouldn't have done that, and it meant Ruth had told her I was in Israel, but Hannah had asked her not to tell me where she was. I asked Ruth if that was the case. She was quiet for a moment, then denied Hannah had done any such thing. Hannah just needed "more time alone, for now," Ruth said, before suggesting I call her back later that day.

I brusquely told Ruth I had to go, and hung up the phone. My whole trip was revealed as a fool's errand. I was angry at Ruth for asking me to go to Israel, and embarrassed I'd ever been gullible enough to agree.

I couldn't be angry with Hannah, but was hurt she wouldn't see me after I'd traveled such a distance. I had two days before my flight back to New York and, now, plenty of free time on my hands. I decided to leave the dust of Jerusalem behind me and, after flipping through the Frommer's guide, booked a cheap hotel in Tel Aviv.

I had no idea what to expect when I got there.

Chapter Sixteen

The "Paradise" in Tel Aviv was just as the Frommer's guide described it, a tired, two-star budget hotel located on a picture-postcard beach, the perfect spot for backpackers. The guide hadn't mentioned the local prostitutes who used the hotel to service mostly college student clients from the U.S. and Europe, in six languages. But for forty dollars a night and a ten percent student discount, who could complain.

I was standing in the lobby waiting to check in when I heard a booming, familiar voice behind me. "Holy shit. Hey, Michael!" It was Dan, the cheerful and slightly chubby lawyer wannabe I'd met four days earlier on the flight to Rome.

"Man, talk about fucking coincidence!" Dan belted out, so loud I was sure everyone in the lobby heard. "I thought you were in Jerusalem the whole week?"

"Dan," I shouted as we proceeded to greet each other with a bear hug, the kind you give an old friend you meet serendipitously in a foreign land otherwise filled with strangers. "I see we bought the same Frommer's guide to Israel," I said. Having spent the last few days alone and depressed I was thrilled to see him.

Dan proceeded to tell me he'd already stayed at the hotel one night, having arrived in Israel late the day before. He'd been checking out the local haunts and was having a blast. And, he said, I wasn't going to believe what went on at the hotel after dark. Extolling the "multilingualism" of a certain group of hotel visitors, he quipped about their ability to "speak in tongues," a performance he'd apparently already experienced personally. It was "gonna be tough getting sleep in this place but it'll be a helluva lot of fun staying awake," he said.

Dan asked me what I'd been up to and I told him I had spent the past three days in Jerusalem, taking copious notes that would prove invaluable for my dissertation. It was a lie, of course, and saying it made me uncomfortable, but I'd gotten used to lying by then. I decided that, even if Dan tortured me, I wouldn't tell him the truth about Hannah and the real purpose of my trip, or why I'd come to Tel Aviv.

Dan tried to persuade me to hit the town with him that night, but I lied again and said I was too tired. As much as I wanted to, I just wasn't up to it. But I told him the next night "for sure," and meant it.

My pre-paid AT&T card was almost used up, but I called Ruth one last time. She told me there had been no news from Hannah. I didn't know whether to believe her and wasn't sure if I cared anymore, but things became somewhat surreal when she asked me, almost too casually, how I was enjoying Israel, what sites I had visited, why I'd gone to Tel Aviv and how it compared to Jerusalem, and, finally, the name and address of my hotel. I found the subject of her curiosities strange given the circumstances, but obliged as best I could—omitting Dan's colorful reporting on the hotel's unique clientele—then told her respectfully—I had never stopped calling her "Mrs. Lindemann"—that I needed to rest and hoped she understood.

Two hours later even the tormented, fitful sleep I'd been enduring the last few months eluded me. Tossing about in bed, sweating profusely in the stifling, airless room, I was nearly delirious, barely able to distinguish reality from illusion. I imagined myself as Nicholas Urfe in Fowles' *The Magus*, the novel with the "indeterminate" ending Hannah insisted I read. I kept asking myself why had she chosen it from among the many dozens of books she could have suggested.

In an almost hallucinatory state, Hannah transmogrified into the beguiling, tripartite Lily/Julie/Vanessa with whom Urfe falls madly, even obsessively in love, only to be repeatedly deceived by her/them; Ruth, into a Maurice Conchis doppelgänger of sorts and master of psychological manipulation. Hadn't Ruth tried to convince Alan that Hannah and I were made for each other despite his apparent desire to come between us, then stood by with seeming indifference for weeks while our love was consumed by the flames of history and memory, only to send me on a wild goose chase to Israel to find the daughter whose very whereabouts oddly remained a mystery to her own mother? I expected at any moment to hear a knock at the door and see Hannah standing there when it opened. She would rush into my arms and we'd make love on the steaming hot bed, then again on a cool stretch of white sand, before she waded alone into the wine dark sea and disappeared once more.

The fever from this delirium had barely passed, and I'd begun to welcome an early semblance of sleep, when I was awakened by a loud banging noise. Still unsure whether I was existing in a dream, reality, or somewhere in between, I opened the door to my room half-believing it would be her. Perhaps, after all my futile searching for Hannah, she had found me and our story would be complete.

She hadn't, and it wasn't. At the door was my newfound friend Dan, accompanied by a lanky Israeli named Eitan.

Chapter Seventeen

Dan was insisting I join Eitan and him for a drink. "Tel Aviv is crazy town, Michael, and you've only got two nights to enjoy it. Just one drink, I promise."

Something told me I wouldn't be able to turn down Dan's invitation. And since the alternative was to spend the rest of the night alone in my room fighting the same demons that his unforeseen intervention had just vanquished, I happily agreed. I shook Eitan's hand in introduction, telling Dan I sorely needed a shower and change of clothes and would meet them both in the lobby in fifteen minutes. I prayed for a second wind.

Exiting the Paradise, we walked a bit before turning on Ben-Yehuda Street, where there were lots of restaurants. I hadn't eaten, and although Dan and Eitan had and were anxious to hit the bars, we soon found a place where I bought and wolfed down a delicious blintz filled with mushrooms, eggplant, and cheese. It really hit the spot.

As we continued in the direction of Dizengoff Square, Dan explained how he had met Eitan in Cairo two days before while visiting al-Azhar Mosque, then described their bus trip across Sinai up to the border crossing at Rafah, the route still littered with blasted tanks from the Yom Kippur War. Eitan was twenty-two and had completed military service a few months earlier, having seen combat in Lebanon. A smattering of conversational Arabic under his belt, Eitan had spent two weeks exploring Egypt, "from Alexandria on down to Aswan," he said. Egypt had opened up to Israeli tourists a year before, one of the benefits of the peace treaty.

Eitan grew up and lived with his parents and a younger brother in Acre, a city a short distance north of Haifa. But he was in no rush to get back home and wasn't starting university until the fall, so after hitting it off with Dan he agreed to spend a few days together with him in Tel Aviv. He and Dan were sharing a double room at the Paradise. The two painted an interesting portrait in contrasts: Dan, a gregarious and light-hearted Jewish-American kid from a well-to-do suburb of Chicago, and Eitan, the taciturn, battle-hardened Sabra.

Before reaching Dizengoff Square—named after Meir Dizengoff, Tel Aviv's famous first mayor from Mandate days—we stopped in a dimly lit pub called the "Milk and Honey" for a quick "kick-off," as Dan described it. Half an hour later, we had already downed two gin and tonics and were working on a first round of Maccabees, the local beer. My head was spinning as the conversation shifted. Dan was reticent to question the reasons for my trip but Eitan sensed the explanations weren't adding up and told me bluntly my story sounded like "bullshit."

"You should work for El Al security, you do a much better job," I quipped, and the three of us burst out laughing.

We shared another hearty laugh after I described my "trial by fire" with Hannah's father, and Dan and Eitan commiserated with me as I confessed my lingering confusion as to Hannah's reasons for breaking up, or why I'd ever gone to Israel in the first place. Dan was empathic, but Eitan once again didn't mince words and said I was a "fool" who never should have come.

"Visit Israel, yes," Eitan said in flawless if accented English, "but not for this reason, not to chase after a woman who doesn't love you." I could hardly dispute his point.

Dan tried to lighten the mood with a silly jingle he must have made up on the spot it was so bad. It went something like "there are plenty of fish in the sea, plenty to catch in the Sea of Galilee." He asked sarcastically whether I had even noticed all of the beautiful Israeli women around us. Dan was right.

There were plenty and I hadn't. We paid our bill and headed off to Dizengoff Square, a bedazzling mixture of Times Square and Greenwich Village, with bright lights, street music, throngs of people, and endless rows of cafes and restaurants. It was Thursday night, the start of the weekend in Israel, and Dizengoff was packed. We found a cafe with an open outside table and ordered up more Maccabees.

It didn't take long for the conversation to turn to the conflict, which, one learns after only a few days in Israel, happens whenever two or more people get together.

Dan started off by asking Eitan if he thought "*we*" were better off having established "*our* security zone" south of the Litani River in Lebanon. I couldn't help but notice Dan's natural, almost instinctive self-identification with Eitan and other Israelis, despite his being an American born and raised in the United States.

"What Americans must understand, especially American Jews," Eitan said, now looking squarely at Dan, "is the nature of the struggle here. It is existential. You know what this word means, existential?" Dan appeared transfixed, Eitan, older than his years.

"The Arabs need peace with Israel more than Israel needs peace with them," Dan said, first raising then nearly slamming his beer bottle on the table, anxious to impress Eitan with his armchair bravado.

"Sadat understood that, and the others will follow ... eventually," Dan continued.

"It cost Sadat his life, Dan," Eitan observed wryly.

Prompted mostly by the desire not to stir potential controversy with my Israeli and Jewish-American interlocutors, I said something trite about "an eye for an eye" making the whole world blind. Eitan raised his hand and shook his finger at me.

"Yes, yes, it may. And I've seen my share of this killing you talk about. I commanded a platoon in Lebanon, and was there from the beginning, the first wave, then, later, up near Beirut. I saw things I cannot describe to you, men, women, children. I cannot speak of it. But I tell you this, there will not be peace here, not for a hundred years, and many, many more will be killed. And so . . ."—Eitan threw up his hands in a manner signifying futility—"we must always be prepared to fight."

As Dan nodded his head in agreement and he and Eitan continued talking, I wondered whether Eitan had been describing, first-hand, his witnessing the aftermath of the massacre at Sabra and Shatila that Alan had asked me about so pointedly. But, while I had opinions about the massacre, and the conflict more broadly—largely informed by the work of Edward Said, a Christian Palestinian who was then a professor of comparative literature at Columbia—I felt in no position to probe Eitan in the same manner.

Said's 1979 book, *The Question of Palestine*, had profoundly influenced my thinking regarding the nature of the conflict, leading me from a Holocaust-centric view that justified the creation of Israel based on the historic crime perpetrated by Germany against the Jews of Europe, to a more holistic and, I believed, more balanced view that took into account the terrible injustice Palestinians had suffered as a result of the establishment of Israel—a forced, often brutal dispossession from their homes and land, which they referred to as the Nakba or Catastrophe, punishment for a crime the Palestinians did not commit.

Hannah and I had discussed Said's book, which included his political and literary critique of *Daniel Deronda*, George Eliot's novel about a Victorian-era gentleman who discovers his Jewish heritage, spurns British aristocratic society to marry a Jewish woman, and leaves England with her on a "journey to the east." Hannah had written a lengthy paper on *Daniel Deronda* in a seminar on politics and literature, and I couldn't help but see parallels between Deronda's personal discovery and journey and Hannah's trip to Israel.

But both the origination point and destination of my own journey into the Middle East maelstrom seemed far less clear. Although Said's writings explored the ideology of Zionism though an intellectual prism, he'd experienced its impact also as a Palestinian whose life, like the lives of hundreds of thousands of other Palestinians, had been negatively and forever affected by it. In contrast, my exploration of Zionism and the conflict had been solely intellectual. I possessed no personal experience or perspective comparable to, or which allowed me to appreciate fully, the suffering Palestinians daily endured as "victims" of Zionism, to use Said's terminology, or, conversely, the powerful appeal of Zionism as "historical idea" to Jews such as Eitan and Dan or, for that matter, Hannah.

As I listened to Eitan and Dan, then, what I heard was Hannah telling me that my not being Jewish meant I could never completely understand Jews' perspectives on antisemitism, the Holocaust, or the conflict, regardless of how much I studied their history. I could no more appropriate that history as my own, I thought, than deny Hannah her understanding of, or connection to it. And so, I remained silent.

I realized what Hannah had tried to convey to me in Memorial Park, which I had failed to fully grasp before that night. Like everyone else, Jews live within history and suffer as individuals. But what Hannah had described was the idea of a shared experience of suffering that almost transcends history, a kind of uber-history binding Jews to one another across cultures, distance, and time. I concluded that Hannah's recent change toward me, her having decided to visit Israel without me, and her refusal even to meet me, meant the power of that idea in her mind had supplanted whatever feelings she once may have had for me in her heart. For of what consequence could the love of one man for a woman be compared to twenty centuries of an ancient people's exile, persecution, and suffering culminating in the ashes of Auschwitz, followed by their redemption and rebirth in a sacred land granted to them by God? There in Dizengoff, it didn't matter to me whether such an idea of history was right or wrong, assuming it could be either. What mattered was I had convinced myself Hannah believed in it, and, as a result, no longer loved me.

Having reached that heartbreaking conclusion about Hannah, and despite Dan and Eitan's companionship and the boisterous crowd around us, I suddenly felt isolated and completely alone. At the very same moment I also felt a certain clearheadedness, like the sobriety that emerges, abruptly but unexpectedly, when the wine you've been drinking no longer clouds your ability to discern what is real and what is not. The overwhelming intoxication brought about by being in Israel, by Jerusalem's mesmerizing exoticness, seemed to dissipate all at once, leaving me stranded between the familiar world from which I had traveled and another I could never hope to truly know, a sojourner in a strange place with limited right of passage but no chance of acceptance, much less permanence, not even through Hannah. In the godforsaken Holy Land sanctified by the blood of Jews and Arabs, I was neither a Jew nor an Arab. I could lay no tribal claim to it, but would remain forever an observer on the outside looking in, a bystander to their *existential* struggle over the same, shattered land, and, now, to Hannah's part in it.

It was, I said to myself at last, time to go home.

Chapter Eighteen

At the next lull in the otherwise spirited conversation between them, I told Dan and Eitan I was going back to the Paradise. I'd decided to cut short my stay in Tel Aviv by a day, and planned to get a hotel Friday night closer to Ben Gurion, as I had an early flight to catch the next morning. It was nearly 2:00 a.m., and I was exhausted. Dan appeared disappointed, but he and Eitan agreed to leave, and we asked for the check.

While we waited, I took out the instant camera I had stuffed in my pocket earlier. I wanted to take a picture of the two of them but Dan got up, grabbed the camera, and said he had a better idea. He walked over to the second table from ours, where a group of three young women were seated, and started talking to one. Apparently, as Eitan was describing Israel's challenges, Dan had a different challenge in mind and had been surveying the feminine horizon across the way.

Amira, the shapely Israeli woman Dan chatted up, walked over to our table with him and, after an awkward moment fumbling with the camera, snapped two pictures of Dan, Eitan, and me, smiling but with eyes half-closed, holding up our last, nearly empty bottles of Maccabees.

Off to the side, Eitan and I whispered to Dan that we weren't interested in having drinks with the three women, and Dan said he would follow us to the hotel shortly. We agreed to meet on the deck behind the Paradise, facing the beach.

On the walk back to the hotel, I was alone with Eitan for the first time that evening. Curious, I asked him what it was like to grow up and live in Israel. Eitan's grandparents had been "Zionist pioneers" who had emigrated from Poland in the 1920s, he recounted. His father was part of the "founding generation" that fought with the Haganah in the 1948 war, and he named his first-born son "Eitan," meaning "strength" in Hebrew.

Shedding his warrior facade suddenly, Eitan told me that, unlike his father, his own experiences in battle had left him deeply troubled and unable to concentrate. He was unusually irritable, argued with his father about the war, and often had nightmares or difficulty sleeping. He went on to explain that although Acre was one of a handful of cities in Israel with a mixed population, Jews and Arabs there lived "mostly separate lives" and always eyed each other "from a distance," with suspicion or worse. "A normal life between us," he appeared to lament, "is very far away."

Eitan's views about Israel's Arabs, and his tone, seemed to me incongruous with his comments earlier that night in Dizengoff, and I told him as much. He had spoken "harshly, like a soldier does," he replied, "to impress Dan." Eitan said Dan idolized him because of his IDF service and combat experience in Lebanon.

"Dan only talks about two things: women and war," Eitan said, chuckling. "He talks to me about the first and wants me to talk to him about the second."

As we waited for Dan on the deck behind the hotel, overlooking the beach, I asked Eitan if he had made Arab friends in school. He explained that in Israel Jews and Arabs go to separate schools—segregated along ethnic lines due to differences in language and culture, and the lingering hostilities from the 1948 war—but that a small number of Arabs attended Jewish schools, mostly those from families seeking to have their children become more integrated into Israeli society.

Eitan's high school had eight Arab students and he'd become friends with one. Hasan was quiet and shy and his father worked, in a clerical capacity of some kind, in a hospital in Acre. He had gone to university after graduation—"Hasan went to college; I went to Lebanon," Eitan groused—and he was studying to become a doctor. Hasan and Eitan had shared an interest in science and a possible career in medicine, but Eitan's own future career now was uncertain.

In a low voice and almost as if it were an afterthought—at least at first it seemed that way to me—Eitan mentioned that he'd also become acquainted at school with Hasan's twin sister, Layal, who he described as a talented artist. I teased Eitan innocently about her, and was surprised when he revealed he'd been taken with Layal, and that meeting her had spurred him to pursue classes in Arabic, which were open to those Jewish students, albeit few in number, interested in learning the language. On a number of occasions, Eitan had "run into Layal" when she was out with Hasan—always in public and "purely by coincidence," he claimed—but their brief encounters ended abruptly after Layal's father, and his own, separately forbade them from seeing each other.

Eitan now expressed mild frustration with Dan and suggested we walk down to the beach without waiting for him. We set off and found a quiet spot. There were a few stragglers sitting and talking nearby, and the pungent smell of marijuana hung in the air. Eitan pulled from his pocket a small pipe and package of tin foil. He opened the foil and broke off a piece of the brown, gummy hashish, filled the pipe and lit it, then took a deep draw. He gave the pipe to me, and I took a long draw and handed it back.

"Lebanese," Eitan said as he exhaled a cloud of smoke, then took a second draw before giving the pipe back to me again. "It's from the Bekaa. Not as good as Moroccan, but still pretty good."

"Seriously good," I said, quickly feeling the effects.

"In Lebanon, everyone smoked. It's how we got through all that *shit*."

The beach was dimly lit by the scattered lights of the few hotel cafes on the promenade that remained open. I sat staring ahead, hypnotized by the nearly still Mediterranean and a low-hanging moon, its pale glow puncturing the darkness and appearing through the mist as a seeping wound in the night sky.

Eitan suddenly broke the silence.

"Do you see her? Is she coming to you in a vision, walking on the water like Jesus on the Sea of Galilee?"

"No," I said, curtly, still staring ahead and piqued that Eitan seemed to be mocking me.

"You know, everyone who comes to Israel is searching for something. When Jews came a hundred years ago, they were looking for their old country. After the war, they came from the camps looking for a new one. American Jews? They come looking to have their picture taken stuffing notes between the stones of the Kotel, so they can go home and tell everyone how much they love Israel. But they leave all the fighting to us."

Eitan let out a bellowing laugh, followed by a smoke-induced cough.

A moment later, he put his arm around my shoulders and turned to me. "Michael, you came to Israel looking for Hannah, but could not find her. For that, my friend, I am sorry." Touched, I reciprocated Eitan's gesture by placing my arm around his shoulders. For several minutes we sat silently together, like that, staring out at the sea and listening to the gentle lap of its waves against the shore.

Dan never joined us on the beach, and after a while Eitan and I shook off the sand from our pants and started back to the Paradise. On the way Eitan again brought up Layal. She was "funny and strong, not afraid to argue with me," he said, and her rare, turquoise-colored eyes, he gushed animatedly, "were like stars up close."

I stopped in my tracks and looked over at Eitan. "Sounds to me like you're in love with her," I said bluntly. "Is there any chance you might get together?"

"There's no chance of that," Eitan replied, his tone now flat and dry as the sand we walked upon.

"Why?" I persisted, naively it would turn out. "You're not teenagers anymore. You're adults."

"This is not possible here," Eitan answered, shaking his head. "On one side of the equation she's an Arab and I'm a Jew. On the other, I'm a Jew and she's an Arab. You understand my meaning, yes?"

I hesitated for just a moment, then nodded in silent affirmation. There was nothing I could say to alter Eitan's seemingly immutable calculus.

"I still think of her sometimes . . . sometimes a lot, sometimes every day maybe," Eitan continued wistfully, a quiet despair in his voice. "But I never want to think about Lebanon again except for Bekaa hashish," he added in quick succession, laughing loudly and patting my shoulder with vigor as we resumed our walk back to the Paradise.

I arranged with Eitan to meet him and Dan in the lobby at ten, so we could have breakfast together in the small cafe next door. I wanted to be sure to say goodbye to the two of them before heading off. At breakfast, Eitan joked about how he'd had to go back to the lobby at three-thirty in the morning and wait a half-hour before returning to the room he was sharing with Dan, because he was still with Amira, the woman who'd taken pictures of the three of us.

Eitan and I shook hands and hugged warmly. I told him he had given me much to think about and hoped our paths would cross again. I gave Dan a bear hug like the one we had greeted each other with the day before. I was going to miss them both.

With a final wave, I walked out the door and made my way to the Tel Aviv bus station. I spent the night nursing a handful of Maccabees in a dingy hotel not far from Ben Gurion Airport, and flew back to the States early the next morning.

~~~

The following week I learned that about an hour after I'd left the Paradise Hannah showed up asking for me. She had called the hotel the night before while I was in Dizengoff Square, but the sleepy or stoned hotel clerk on duty at two in the morning had never given me the message.

Chapter Nineteen

Pat had my return flight information and picked me up at JFK. Although the flight to Rome departed on time, the charter from Rome to New York ended up leaving four hours late so he'd been waiting for close to five hours before I finally emerged from the arrivals hall with my backpack and crumpled copy of the International Herald Tribune in hand, grateful to see him.

"Long trip," Pat said, "you must be exhausted."

"Long wait. *You* must be exhausted," I replied.

I spent the ride telling Pat everything that had happened in Israel, and how it seemed clear Hannah and I were finished. Pat first played devil's advocate, then shifted, with equal lack of success, to the "more fish in the sea" approach Dan had tried out on me. He ended with a philosophical—perhaps theological is the better word—flourish about fate and how we must resign ourselves to it. He assured me that "God has a plan for everyone," a sort of Catholic *beshert* doctrine.

When we arrived at my building, I asked Pat if he wanted to come up to the apartment, but he declined since it was already late and he had a long ride back to Yonkers, where in a few weeks he would be starting his third year of seminary training. I thanked him effusively, telling him he'd gone above and beyond the call of duty for waiting for me so long.

I threw my backpack in the corner of the room, along with the small satchel bag I had taken with me, now filled with guidebooks, my passport, some clipped bus and entrance tickets, and the two instant cameras used on the trip. I fell on my bed and almost immediately into a deep sleep.

Two days later, I received a note from Ruth thanking me "ever so much for going to Israel to give me peace of mind about Hannah" and expressing how sorry she was Hannah and I hadn't been able to see each other while I was there. She wrote that she had given Hannah the name of the Paradise and understood she'd gone to see me Friday morning, but that I'd already left. I put down the card and shook my head, recalling what Pat had said to me about fate.

Ruth ended by saying she hoped to see me again "soon." I put the note back in its envelope and placed it in the satchel bag along with the other things from the trip.

A letter from Hannah, postmarked the day after I left Israel, arrived about a week later. She wrote me, as Ruth already had, that she'd gone to the Paradise that Friday morning but was told I'd checked out. She went on to say she'd been shocked to hear I'd gone all the way to Israel, and that there was never a reason to go because she had a "smart head" on her shoulders and knew perfectly well how to take care of herself. But, she added, she had been "genuinely touched" by my "thoughtfulness." She concluded by saying she'd have a lot to tell me when she returned.

A post card followed in early July, then a long letter that arrived the very beginning of August. In it Hannah explained at length how she'd been traveling the country for six weeks, had made friends with several Americans who'd made aliyah, and had decided to move to Israel "temporarily" to explore whether a permanent move was what she really wanted. Making aliyah was a process and it took several months to obtain necessary approvals through the Jewish Agency. In the meantime, she'd withdrawn from the student teaching spot she had lined up as part of her master's program, secured a temporary teaching position in Haifa, and would begin a crash course in Hebrew. She was "so excited" and hoped I understood what this "new stage in my life" meant to her. In addition to the job, she'd arranged an apartment share with a friend, Margalit, who was from Boston and had made aliyah the year before. Hannah told me her father was "thrilled" about her move to Israel, Ruth less so but she remained "supportive."

Hannah returned to New Jersey for two weeks around the end of August to finalize arrangements. We met for lunch, then took a long walk in Riverside Park, our path following the southward course of the Hudson. We hadn't seen each other since mid-May, and at first the almost business-like encounter felt surreal given the intensity of our feelings for one another just a few months before. Although I said nothing about it, I also couldn't help notice that Hannah wasn't wearing the necklace I'd given her; it was the first time I'd seen her without it since her birthday in October.

After listening to Hannah talk about Israel for two hours, I decided to force the issue of our relationship.

"What does this mean for us, Hannah? You know how much I love you, but I don't know how you feel about me, about us. It's been months since we've been together, or really talked. I can't ask you not to go to Israel if that's where your heart is leading you. But I can't move there. I'm just starting my dissertation work at Columbia, and can't just leave my family. They would never understand it. I'm honestly not sure you'd want me to go even if I could."

"Something is pulling me to Israel, Michael, something I can't fully explain or resist. That I don't want to resist, frankly. So much has happened over the past few months. This is not about you, or the letter, if that's what you're thinking. And I need to figure it out alone. I can't commit to anything about us right now, and it wouldn't be fair for me to tell you otherwise."

I was thinking about the letter, but didn't want to bring it up. I understood Hannah's desire to explore making aliyah to Israel. What I couldn't understand was her apparent indifference to leaving me behind. Everything seemed to have changed after Memorial Park, and I had no satisfactory explanation as to why.

"I'm not asking you to commit to anything, Hannah, but I need you to be honest about how you feel."

"I am being honest about what I've been feeling, Michael." Hannah paused, lowering her head for a moment before engaging my eyes again. "I love you. That hasn't changed. But other things have. I need three or four months to decide what to do, whether I want to make aliyah."

"*Whether* you want to? Hannah, you gave up Columbia, your teaching placement. You're learning Hebrew, and you got an apartment and a job in Haifa."

"It's a *temporary* position," Hannah insisted.

"Hannah, you don't need my approval for moving to Israel, if that's what you want to do. But you're making a decision for both of us. I don't see any way forward for *us* if this happens. Do you? It means the end of everything we've had together. Do you honestly see things differently?"

Hannah lowered her head slightly, then, lifting it, took my hands in her own. I felt an adrenaline rush from her touch; it had been the subject of my longing for months. In a hushed voice, she said she still loved me, but couldn't "predict" what her moving to Israel would mean for the two of us. I closed my eyes, and held them shut for a long moment. Her answer was the one I'd been expecting, but dreading. There was no longer any doubt in my mind that Hannah's move wasn't going to be temporary. She'd decided to make aliyah, but appeared unable to bring herself to telling me.

I cradled Hannah's face gently with my hands, and kissed her for what would be the last time. Not with passion, as I had so many times before, but resignation. I didn't think there was anything more I could do or say to resolve whatever issues Hannah had with me, or her grandmother, or with history. I didn't even know what they were because she hadn't told me. I believed Hannah when she said she loved me, and I wanted desperately to save our relationship, but felt the only choice I had given hers was to step back and let go. Was it because I hoped that with enough time to explore what she needed to in Israel Hannah would want me to be a part of her life again, or because I knew deeper in my heart that, despite whatever love of hers for me remained, she would not? I pretended not to know which it was.

But when Hannah and I hugged each other to say goodbye, the feeling of distance between us was unmistakable, a frightful, dreamlike sense of falling through the air with no one there to catch you, of putting your arms around the person you've loved more than anyone and seeking singularity but finding only emptiness, a void that leaves you standing alone even when you're together, two people occupying the same space yet in different places.

Hannah had already left me. I'd lost her forever.

~~~

Hannah wrote to me about a month after her arrival in Israel. She missed our "friendship a great deal" and wanted me to know she still "cared for me deeply." The letter went on to tell me about all the historic places she'd visited, her new apartment, the "amazing" bus system, new friends she was making, the "exciting new feelings" she was having, and how she was "truly in love with this place." She said she'd write again soon.

I tore up Hannah's letter into tiny pieces and let them fall to the ground. It wasn't anger so much as the desire to erase Hannah's words, all the details of a new and different life that she would never share with me.

Hannah wrote again during the fall and even asked me to visit her. I looked into the fares but decided not to go, and never did answer her letters. I preferred not to visit Israel as a tourist again now that Hannah had decided to move there permanently, and couldn't bear the thought of saying goodbye to her for a second time. After a while, her letters started arriving further and further apart, and by mid-winter they stopped altogether.

~~~

About two years after Hannah made aliyah, I ran into Gary at "No Name," a quirky bar on Fifth Avenue a few blocks north of Washington Square Park, which I used to frequent while attending NYU. A group of my NYU friends had gathered there for a reunion and invited me. I hadn't spoken to Gary since dropping him at home more than three years before, following the Model UN conference. I wasn't surprised to hear that he was still in touch with Vania, our friend from Brazil, and still trying to convince her to date him. Gary said Vania had become friends with Jillian, Hannah's old roommate from UPenn, who now worked in the city. He told me Vania had learned through Jillian that Hannah had gotten married in Israel a month before.

Later that night and after drinking far more than I should, I returned to my apartment and lay on the bed, my thoughts racing through time, back to

Pelham Bay and the Christmas fire, to Princeton and the Cloisters, to that awful afternoon in Memorial Park. I remembered the trip to Israel and wondered whether things might have turned out differently if I hadn't written that letter and argued with Hannah about it, or rushed to leave Tel Aviv the morning after my night out with Dan and Eitan in Dizengoff Square. All I knew for certain about Hannah and me was that our story had come to an end two years earlier, and there was nothing "indeterminate" about it.

Five years would pass before I learned I had been wrong.

Part Three

1990

Chapter Twenty

The Lord said unto Moses: "Consecrate to me all the firstborn; whatever is the first to open the womb among the Israelites . . . is mine."

Exodus 13:2

Without a word he . . . bound Issac, and without a word he unsheathed his knife. Then he beheld the ram God had chosen, and sacrificed him, and wended his way home. . . . From that day on Abraham grew old. He could not forget that God had required this of him. Issac flourished as before; but Abraham's eye was darkened, he saw happiness no more.

Søren Kierkegaard
Fear and Trembling

B ack at the apartment after returning from the Bronx, I frantically dialed Pat's number the minute I hung up from Ruth.

"Pick up the phone, Pat, pick up the goddamn phone."

"Hello," Pat finally answered, desultorily, after the sixth ring.

"She's dead, Pat. Hannah's dead."

I was shouting and could hardly believe what I was saying.

"I need to borrow your car. I've got to see Hannah's mother tomorrow in New Jersey."

"Holy Jesus, Michael, how? What happened?"

Stunned and still trembling from the news, I proceeded to relay to Pat what Ruth had told me a few minutes before. Hannah had been killed in a freakish accident three months earlier, in Haifa. An elderly American tourist, who almost certainly shouldn't have been driving, had swerved his rental car suddenly and sharply to the right to avoid a Vespa passing him on the left, and had hit Hannah as she was waiting for the bus to go home from the school where she taught. Two others had been injured, but Hannah had been pinned under the car and suffered massive internal bleeding. She'd left behind her husband, Matt, and two children, a nearly four-year-old son, Joshua, and a two-year-old daughter, Ruth, named after her grandmother.

Ruth had asked me if I might be willing to come see her, and I told her I'd be there the next day. I needed to borrow Pat's car because my father had sold the old Skylark when he moved near my sister. Around eleven the next morning, and after a sleepless night, Pat picked me up near Xavier; I had called in sick a few hours before. Once Pat drove us back to his apartment in Yonkers, I took the car out to Maplewood. I stopped first at the bakery near Pat's place to pick up a small coffee cake. I didn't know what else to bring.

Hannah's house was as I remembered it, a neat Dutch colonial on a quarter acre lot, with an ascending front lawn and five guard-railed steps leading up to the front door. Only the color had changed, from pale green to a vibrant yellow. I knocked, holding the coffee cake. As I waited, I noticed the mezuzah on the right side of the door, about a third of the way down its length, recalling how when entering the house ahead of me Hannah would touch it and quietly recite the blessing. I suddenly felt impelled to place my own hand on it, not in obedience to any Halakic injunction but by the deluded hope that I might feel some corporeal connection to Hannah through it. After I did, though, I felt nothing, only the touch of cold metal.

A handful of seconds later, the door opened and Ruth appeared. She looked much the same except for salt and pepper hair that had turned an ashen grey. Tilting her head down toward me, she displayed mournful eyes but the same warm smile I remembered.

"Michael," she said, "thank you so much for coming."

"Mrs. Lindemann," I said, my voice cracking, "I am so sorry."

Ruth reached out to hug me, and we embraced in the doorway for a long moment tinged with grief. She led me inside, through the hallway and into the dining room where the five of us had Shabbos dinner nearly eight years before. On one end of the credenza was a picture of Ruth, Alan, and Hannah, taken at her graduation from UPenn, alongside one of Hannah, Matt, Joshua, and little Ruth. There was also a picture of Hannah from her Bat Mitzvah, when she would have been about twelve. She looked the same as I remembered her that wintry night outside Zelda's hat shop.

We entered the living room together, and Ruth motioned for me to sit down and make myself comfortable. The couch was still positioned across the two arm chairs that Alan and Zelda had sat in that night after dinner, a coffee table between the couch and the chairs. The room almost seemed to have been frozen in time. In the center of the table there was a decorative bowl, flanked on each side by stacks of books, on the top of one stack a thick volume entitled, *Jews in Germany: From Roman Times to the Weimar Republic.* There was also a soft, brown leather case.

"Let me cut us some of this yummy-looking cake, Michael. What can I get you? Do you still drink tea with lemon? I've started to make some."

"Yes, thanks, that would be fine," I said. "It's a habit Hannah got me into years ago, and I can't seem to break it. But only if it's not too much trouble and you're making some for yourself."

Sitting in that familiar spot, I realized I'd neither seen Alan nor asked Ruth about him. When she returned with a tray filled with a tea pot, cups, and cake, I asked whether Alan was working or, perhaps, had retired early. Ruth told me he had passed away two years before, just weeks prior to little Ruth being born and following a short—six month—battle with pancreatic cancer. For a second time, I expressed my condolences to her. Ruth was alone now, she said, except for Matt and the grandchildren. She had stopped working at the Manhattan law firm soon after Alan's death, and volunteered at the town library four days a week.

Ruth recounted to me again how the person who'd hit Hannah hadn't been charged criminally because he had swerved abruptly to avoid the Vespa. Although Matt might eventually look into a negligence suit, according to the police report and local newspapers, Hannah had been killed in a "tragic accident."

Pouring each of us a cup of tea, Ruth began describing Hannah's life over the preceding seven years. She told me Hannah had decided in 1984 to settle near Haifa—for reasons she'd "explain shortly" she said—and once settled she started teaching English language and literature courses in a local high school. She met Matt, a "kind and wonderful man," the same year. Matt was two years older than Hannah and originally from Rochester, New York. He'd made aliyah after graduating college in 1980, served in the IDF for the required stint—as a woman making aliyah Hannah had been exempt from military service—then started teaching physics at the school where Hannah taught, which is where they met. They were married in 1985, and "rambunctious" Joshua arrived about a year later. "Little baby Ruth," a "precocious child like her grandmother," was born two years after that. Hannah was on her way to pick them up when it happened.

Hannah's death had left Ruth "devastated," and her summary of Hannah's life in Israel was punctuated by tearful fits and starts. Inconsolable until recently, she said, she had begun coming to terms with the reality and finality of it all only in the last few days.

"Michael, it's been a long time, but I felt you'd want to know what had happened to Hannah. I know how much you meant to each other once."

"Hannah certainly meant a great deal to me," I said, changing slightly the premise of Ruth's remark.

"Michael, I asked if you could come for another reason as well. I wanted to let you know about Hannah. But I also think it's important for you to understand what happened seven years ago. I don't believe you ever had the full picture."

"What do you mean?" I asked.

"That day the two of you argued at Memorial Park—yes, Hannah's father and I heard all about it— Hannah was very upset about something and I think it may have started a chain of events."

"I know she was very upset about her grandmother, and I never should have . . ."

Ruth interrupted me. "Zelda was *not* Hannah's grandmother."

"What?" I said, shocked. It was the last thing I expected to hear. "I'm not sure I understand, Mrs. Lindemann."

"Michael, please, call me Ruth, especially after all these years."

"Ruth," I repeated her name slowly, "I'm a little confused right now."

"It's a long story," Ruth said, pointing to the leather case on the table. "Let's have some more tea." Ruth poured each of us a second cup and took a few sips. I mimicked her, but without swallowing, anxious to hear what she was going to say. Ruth leaned slightly forward in the armchair and placed her hands on her knees, the blue, neatly buttoned dress she wore falling just below them.

"Are you comfortable, Michael?" she asked.

"Yes," I said. "But if Zelda wasn't Hannah's grandmother . . ."

"That's right, Zelda was not my mother.

"Zelda Manzbach was my aunt, my mother's younger sister. My mother was Hanna Manzbach. I named Hannah after her. My mother's family lived in Munich before the war. My mother was born in 1912, and my Aunt Zelda in 1914. My grandfather was Walter Manzbach, and he fought for Germany in World War I. After the war ended, and shortly after my grandmother died in 1922, my grandfather took over his father's hat manufacturing business. It had been started a few decades earlier when the family moved to Munich. The factory was one of the largest in the country, and the hats were sold all over Germany.

"My mother attended the University of Munich. My Aunt Zelda was quiet and shy and after completing *gymnasium*, similar to high school, she went to work for my grandfather's business, handling the accounts. It was known as *Manzbach Hutfabrik*. How's your German, Michael?"

"I learned to read a bit for graduate school, but I'm pretty rusty now."

"By the way, did you ever get your . . ."

"That's a story for another day," I interjected as quickly as I could, before segueing back to Zelda.

"Hannah once told me that her grandmother, ah, that Zelda used to go to her father's hat factory after school to help her father and that they would walk home together, just like she did with Zelda in the Bronx."

"Yes, that's true. My mother, on the other hand, wasn't interested in hats. She was, however, a brilliant student of Jewish history and foreign languages, and a very determined woman. Let me show you some pictures."

Ruth leaned over and opened the leather case, removing an envelope that contained what appeared to be a few dozen vintage photographs of her family from the years before the Second World War. There was one from 1928 of Ruth's grandfather, Walter, a handsome but stern figure seated with Zelda and Hanna, Ruth's mother, standing alongside him. Both sisters were wearing long formal dresses and smiling, Zelda straight ahead into the camera, and Hanna Manzbach looking and smiling dreamily off to the right.

Another was a close-up of the two sisters, each wearing a white, collared dress tightly buttoned up to their necks, with black hair parted down the middle and pulled back. Zelda had large, wide-open eyes conveying a benign gentleness beneath bushy eyebrows; Hanna's eyes were almond-shaped and piercing.

The photo I remember most vividly was one of Hanna Manzbach standing alone and against a white background. She was wearing a plaid dress with a slim, corseted waist wrapped tight around and up to her bosom, the collar closed off by a large brooch. Her hair, full and shoulder length in the photo taken with Zelda, was here cut short and combed back; she almost resembled a man. Hanna's eyes stared off to her right with a determined, resolute gaze. The inked notation on the bottom of the photo read, "Hanna Manzbach, Jerusalem, Palestine, 1937."

"Hanna," Ruth explained to me, was a German spelling of Hannah, derived from Johanna, itself the romanized version of Yohannah, a female Hebrew name originating from the masculine, Yehohanan, meaning "God is gracious."

"Wait," I said, "Jerusalem, Palestine, 1937?"

"Everything I'm about to tell you is what I was told by my Aunt Zelda, and learned from reading the dozens of letters she saved," Ruth replied, pointing to the bundle on the table. "Letters to and from my mother after . . . let me stop there, I'm getting ahead of myself.

"My mother loved reading history and studying foreign languages, and was fluent in Yiddish, Russian, Polish, and French. She wanted to pursue a graduate degree, which was somewhat uncommon for women. Now, like many assimilated German-Jewish families, my grandfather's household was not very religious. The family attended synagogue on the High Holy Days, but didn't keep kosher or regularly observe the Sabbath. They celebrated Christmas, and had a Christmas tree like other Germans; most German Jews did the same.

"My mother believed that assimilation into German society and culture was a betrayal of Jewish history and culture. She supported the Zionist movement as a means to achieve Jewish renewal in our homeland Eretz Israel. My grandfather, however, was quite opposed to the Zionists. He believed the movement risked the social, cultural, and economic gains Jews had made in Germany over centuries.

"My mother had started to become involved in Zionist youth groups from her time in *gymnasium*. She was a member of several, Youth Aliyah, Blue and White Ramblers, and one called 'Kadima,' which in Hebrew means 'Forward.' Answering this yearning in her heart, my mother started planning to make aliyah to Palestine. Beginning in the 1920s, thousands of German Jews did the same. Something like sixty thousand emigrated from Germany to Palestine during the 1920s and 1930s in what became known as the Fifth Aliyah.

"While all this was happening, however, my mother fell in love with a man named Stefan Reiner. She had known him since they were teenagers because he was the son of one of my grandfather's suppliers. They attended the University of Munich, where they studied history, and each wanted to pursue graduate degrees. Stefan was Catholic, but his academic interest was Jewish history, in particular the earliest settlements of Jews in Germany. It was unusual at the time for gentile Germans to be students of Jewish history. He and my mother shared this interest and were drawn to each other."

"You're talking now about 1932, 1933, when Hitler came to power?"

"Yes, my mother and Stefan received their undergraduate degrees in 1934, just a year after all Jewish professors were dismissed from the universities. They became very close and talked of marriage, but my mother remained active in the youth groups and held on to this deep desire to make aliyah to Palestine."

"Did Stefan know how strongly she felt about this?"

"According to Zelda, my mother spoke to my grandfather and Stefan about emigrating. My grandfather couldn't understand why she'd risk losing what the family had built up in Germany, and apparently he and my mother had terrible arguments. Stefan asked my mother to marry, and my grandfather encouraged it, thinking it would put an end to her desire to emigrate. He felt Stefan was from a respectable family—he knew his father very well—and that a marriage would be good for the family business. But my mother turned him down.

"In 1935, my mother applied to the Jewish Agency in Munich and received approval for an immigration certificate allowing her to go to Palestine. After several months of agricultural training required by the Jewish Agency, she was issued the certificate and returned to Munich to prepare for the journey. She spent much of those last few weeks with Stefan. He tried to convince her not to go, and again asked her to marry him. But my mother turned him down again, refusing to change her mind about Palestine. At the end of those weeks, she left, taking the train to Trieste and traveling by sea to Jaffa. Soon after arriving in Palestine, however, she discovered she was pregnant."

"Okay, I now understand where this is going. Was it . . . ?"

"Yes. Stefan Reiner was my father. My mother wrote to him to explain that she loved him and was carrying his child, but her desire to live in Palestine was the fulfillment of a lifelong dream and, she said, part of the 'historical destiny of the Jewish people.' She knew, she wrote, that he would understand what making aliyah meant to her. It's in there with the other letters because my father gave Zelda the ones my mother sent him. She told my father she was committed to raising me as 'a proud Jew in the land of our forefathers.' While pregnant with me she lived in an immigrant hostel with other German Jews she'd traveled with to Palestine."

"But I thought your mother loved Stefan?"

"I can never know what she truly felt in her heart. She told Zelda, as she had my father, that she loved him, but said that marriage was impossible because of the Nuremberg Laws enacted in September 1935. That much was true. She also knew that knowledge my father had a child with a Jewish woman would destroy any hope of an academic career for him."

Ruth leaned over to pick up the leather case and began rifling through the old photos looking for one of her father.

"Here he is. This was my father, Stefan Reiner."

Ruth handed me the photo. I studied Stefan's features carefully. He was tall and dressed handsomely in traditional Bavarian clothing, his blonde, wavy hair parted down the middle. He wore dark, horn-rimmed glasses and was smiling broadly as he and Zelda stood close to each other, his arms extended around her waist.

"Is that Zelda?" I asked, already knowing the answer.

"Yes, they became very close after my mother left for Palestine, and given everything they had to deal with together."

"Did Zelda fall in love with your father?" I asked, thinking a moment later that I had overstepped.

"Sometimes I believe she did fall in love with him, although she never said that to me. Still, at times over the years she expressed bitterness toward my mother for how she'd treated my father, for the decisions she made that led to everything. Maybe that was her way of telling me she loved him, I don't know." Ruth paused for a moment. "But this was so many years ago, all in the past."

Ruth waved the photo in the air, then placed it back in its envelope in the leather case. She appeared flummoxed, as if she'd lost her train of thought.

"Now, you've distracted me, Michael," Ruth chided lightheartedly.

"So, getting back to the story, my mother had confided in Zelda about the pregnancy, but swore her to secrecy. My grandfather only knew that my mother had gone to Palestine. The Nuremberg Laws made it illegal for an Aryan German to marry a Jew, and stripped German Jews of citizenship, making them 'subjects' of the Reich. Even if a mixed couple were married abroad, the marriage would not have been valid in Germany, so my father's traveling to Palestine to marry my mother and their returning home together was never an option. In fact, both were subject to criminal prosecution. All that, and my mother's desire to remain in Palestine, created the dilemma."

"So what happened? You were born in Palestine?"

"Yes, I was born in Haifa, on August 3, 1936. Because I was born after July 31 of that year, as a result of my father's extramarital relationship with a Jewish woman, I was considered a Jew for purposes of the Nuremberg Laws.

"My aunt soon started receiving letters from my mother describing the difficulties she faced not only as an unwed mother of an unexpected child, but as a new immigrant. In Palestine, German-Jewish immigrants were called 'yekkes'. While in Germany, Germans considered them Jews, in Palestine the Jews who had settled there before considered the new arrivals Germans. The German Jews couldn't speak or read Hebrew and few apparently made the effort. They retained their intellectual interests, cultural attitudes, eating habits, even their dress, and that bred resentment among the Jews who'd immigrated years earlier. There was also animosity because many felt the German Jews arriving in the mid-1930s had gone to Palestine only to escape Hitler, not to settle the land as they had, as committed Zionist pioneers."

"How long did you live in Palestine?"

"After a time on a kibbutz further to the north, my mother settled us back in Haifa where many German-Jewish immigrants lived. Because of her language skills, she was able to get a job translating and writing for German and Yiddish newspapers, and I spent my days in community nurseries. But life was difficult for my mother. Friends and neighbors were aware I'd been born out of wedlock, and that my father was a gentile. She developed malaria, then dysentery. This went on for about two years, and as my mother got weaker physically her mental condition also began to deteriorate. All the while she had no family support to help raise me."

"Was Stefan aware of all this?"

"Yes, Zelda showed him my mother's letters. He told her he still loved my mother and wanted to marry her, but felt there was nothing he could do as she refused to return to Germany, and he was not prepared to leave behind his family. And, of course, the situation was getting worse for Jews, so it was never a realistic option. Jews were trying to get out of Germany, not return to it. Then, in November 1938, on Kristallnacht, all hell broke loose.

"Like many German Jews, my grandfather had seen it coming. In late 1935, after passage of the Nuremberg Laws, he applied for three visas to immigrate to America, including one for my mother. At my grandfather's insistence my mother signed the visa papers just before leaving for Palestine. There were strict quotas limiting the number of visas and he had to renew the applications twice, in 1936 and again in 1937. It was my grandfather's hope that if the visas were granted my mother would leave Palestine and go with him and my Aunt Zelda to America, where he planned to start a new business. By 1937, his sales had fallen nearly by half because of the Nazi boycott. Then, on Kristallnacht, the hat factory was torched and partly burned down. A few years later it would be confiscated and converted into a factory for making uniforms and boots. The Nazis demanded the insurance payments received by Jewish businesses that had been destroyed, claiming the Jews had instigated the violence, but the insurance companies refused to go along with the sham and paid the claims for the sake of their business reputations. The Nazis got around it by assessing massive fines against the owners, including my grandfather.

"By the end of 1938, it became clear from my mother's letters that she was no longer able to care for me. She was physically ill and becoming more and more depressed. She lost her job translating and writing for the German newspapers, and so was deprived even of that meager income. My aunt sent her money from what she earned at the hat factory. In one of my mother's letters, from December 1938, she told my Aunt Zelda she was considering placing me in an orphanage. Zelda wrote back begging her not to, and asked her to consider leaving Palestine and traveling to a third country where she could be reunited with her, or with Stefan. Zelda told my mother about my grandfather's plans to emigrate and that the visa applications had been granted. But my mother refused to leave Palestine. She asked my Aunt Zelda to take me."

"What happened?"

"Zelda told my father, and the two devised a plan. On the pretense of seeking material from Oxford University for his research, my father struck up a friendship with a young consular officer in the British Consulate in Munich, a fellow named Harry Stanton. It was Stanton who gave my father the idea of how to get me out of Palestine.

"What Stanton said was that my father could apply for a temporary permit to visit Palestine and claim paternity. Because I'd been born there and my mother had a certificate of Palestine citizenship issued by the British Mandate authorities, we were Palestine nationals and could get documents allowing us to travel under the protection of the British government. My father would return to Germany with me, and my grandfather and Aunt Zelda could then immediately apply for three transit visas to England.

"The transit visas allowed people who had applied for visas from third countries to stay in England temporarily while waiting to receive final approval. Since my grandfather had already received the approvals from the U.S. Consulate and was on a waiting list for issuance of the visas, Stanton believed the British Consulate would approve three transit visas, including one for me. Stanton told my father he would do what he could to make sure of it, and he turned out to be true to his word.

"My father obtained the necessary permit in Munich and traveled to Jaffa, taking the same route my mother had about three years before. He went to Haifa where we were living, and, according to the description he later gave Zelda, my mother spoke about reuniting with him, her, and me in Palestine after things settled down in Europe. It was delusional. She agreed to marry my father to allow him to claim paternity and get me out of Palestine and to Germany. A British consular officer conducted a civil ceremony, as Stanton had suggested.

"My father stayed in Palestine for nearly three months, to arrange the legal proceedings to document his paternity and the marriage to my mother, and to obtain a passport for me. Because I had been born in Haifa, I was a citizen of Palestine and could be issued a British passport.

"Once the legal proceedings were completed, my father went to the German Consulate in Jerusalem to obtain a travel permit allowing me to enter Germany. Perhaps because my father told them that after arriving in Germany I would immediately leave to go to England with my aunt, they issued an entry visa and my father took me back. Neither my father nor I would ever see my mother again."

Ruth picked up the leather case, and after a moment rummaging though it pulled out a small, brown booklet, labeled "BRITISH PASSPORT" with the word "PALESTINE" written directly beneath. Inside was a photo of Ruth as a child, identifying her as "Rúth Sarah Reiner." She pointed out the page containing the entry visa stamped by the German Consulate in Jerusalem.

Ruth explained to me that, by Nazi decree in 1938, all German Jews whose first names did not appear on the official, published "Jewish list" of names, including German Jews in Palestine holding German passports, were required to add "Israel" or "Sarah" as a middle name to identify them as Jews. Even infants born to German Jews in Palestine were subject to the order, and the Consulate had to attest to the change so that the police in the parents' home town could record the birth. The German Consulate told Stefan that his marriage to Ruth's mother would not be recognized as valid in Germany, but nevertheless required him to record the name change for Ruth before issuing the entry visa. Doing so had resulted in a delay of several weeks. Although Hebrew in origin, the name "Ruth" had become sufficiently "Germanized" and so did not appear on the "Jewish list," necessitating the addition of "Sarah" to Ruth's visa papers and passport. This was done, Ruth said, to ensure that so long as she remained in Germany, and consistent with the Nuremberg Laws, she would be identified as a Jew.

"Once we finally arrived in Germany, my grandfather was able to get the three transit visas, and we left for England a few weeks later. Zelda told him everything, and I'm sure it broke his heart a second time as he had hoped my mother would be returning to Germany with me. It was April 1939. The U.S. visas, including one for me originally approved for my mother, were issued two months later. In July, just a few months before the war started, we set sail for America on a steamship from the Port of Southampton. We were fortunate. Especially after Kristallnacht, tens of thousands of German Jews sought to immigrate to the U.S., but by then visas were virtually impossible to come by. My grandfather's foresight saved us. Nearly a third of the five hundred thousand or so Jews who lived in Germany when Hitler came to power never made it out, and many of those didn't survive the camps, including my uncle and his entire family. We arrived in America with hardly any money. The Nazis forced my grandfather to pay a large exit fee to leave."

"And your mother?"

"My mother's mental state continued to deteriorate. Her letters over the next two years displayed an almost manic range of emotions, sometimes complaining in detail about the slights of friends and neighbors, other times writing in glowing terms about her life in the Yishuv. But by 1941, she was severely depressed and seemed to be losing grip with reality. In her last few letters she appeared to have become obsessed with a woman she'd read about who had immigrated with her husband to Jerusalem in the 1860s."

Ruth stood and leaned over to pick up the bundle of old letters on the table, now yellowed with age. They had been placed in strict chronological order.

"I've read every one of these many times," Ruth said.

"This is the last one. My mother is writing about Rivkah Lipa Anikster, who together with her husband left seven children behind in Europe to make aliyah to Jerusalem, where she died in 1893. She had written a pamphlet that my mother had read and she wrote about it to my Aunt Zelda. It was called *Zekher Olam, For Eternal Memory*."

After reading aloud in German, Ruth translated for me. "What a sacrifice this woman made for the sake of Eretz Israel, granting her seven children long life. Just like my sacrifice in giving precious little Ruth over to your tender hands, while I remain here to bring renewed life to the land of our fathers. Listen to Rivkah's words: 'You should know, my beloved children, that our journey to the Holy City of Jerusalem was very difficult, it was a test like the binding of the Patriarch Issac.' Dearest sister, my journey has been Rivkah's journey."

Ruth placed the letter down on the table.

"That's what my mother wrote, her journey had been Rivkah's. My mother identified with a woman who'd abandoned her seven children to make aliyah to Jerusalem and compared what she'd done to the binding of Issac, to Abraham's willingness to sacrifice his son at God's command. My mother believed the same was true about me, that she had given me up as a sacrifice demanded by God."

Ruth paused and seemed on the verge of tears. I offered to get her a glass of water and ran to the kitchen. She was composed when I got back, but took several sips. She folded and carefully placed the letter back into the leather case.

"What happened to your mother?" I asked, trepidation in my voice.

Ruth stared at me, her eyes still welled with tears.

"My mother took her life, on August 3, 1941, my fifth birthday. Neighbors found her in the apartment. She had hanged herself. We don't know exactly what led to it. Maybe she was despondent over having given me up and feared she'd never see me again. Maybe the struggle of living alone and her depression finally caught up to her. I'll never know. With the war, communications were hard. She hadn't written to Zelda in months, and didn't leave a note. She was twenty-nine, the same age as Hannah when she died. She's buried in Haifa. That's where my Aunt Zelda and I went the day Hannah toured Masada with her father. I told Hannah we were staying back at the hotel because the trip would be too grueling for her *grandmother*, but we took a taxi to the cemetery in Haifa. Zelda wanted to visit her sister's grave before she died. I'd never returned since leaving in 1939, and, of course, I wanted to visit the grave of my mother for the first time, to recite *El Maleh Rahamim* for her, our prayer for the soul of the dead."

"I am so sorry Ruth." I found myself expressing condolences to Ruth for the third time in a single day.

But there was more to come.

Chapter Twenty-One

"And your father," I asked, nervously. "What happened to him?"

"My father remained in Germany. Nazi efficiency being what it was, the Jerusalem Consulate had alerted the police in Munich. There was a special unit that investigated violations of the Nuremberg Laws. He was interrogated for two days. Since he'd claimed paternity in Jerusalem he had no choice but to confess to *Rassenschande*, the crime of 'race defilement.'"

"Was he sent to prison?"

"That was usually the case, but no. The Nazis investigated but didn't prosecute him. It might have been the influence of his father, my paternal grandfather, who was a major raw materials supplier and ended up being forced to convert his factories to wartime production. I don't know. What I know is that the Nazis considered a Jewish man having relations with a German woman an offense against German blood and honor. What my father had done was considered an offense only against German honor. Perhaps that's why he wasn't sent to prison. Perhaps they wanted him to serve in the army. I'll never know for sure.

"His academic career, however, was ruined, as my mother had predicted. He had already suffered as a result of the rumors. His professors and many of his peers knew about his relationship with my mother back in 1936, and that she was Jewish and had gone to Palestine. Then, when my father traveled to Palestine their suspicions were raised, only to have them confirmed when he brought back his three-year old child. It was scandalous, and very dangerous for him.

"The university had never approved his doctorate even as late as 1938, and he now had no hope of finding a position in Germany. For decades before the war there had been a movement in German-Jewish circles known as *Wissenschaft des Judentums*. The idea was to study Judaism, and Jewish history and culture, in a scientific manner. There were institutes filled with German-Jewish scholars, the most prominent being the Academy for the Scientific Study of Judaism in Berlin.

"But the Nazis were trying to develop their own scholarly foundation for their racist views of Jews. In studying the 'Jewish Question' historians at the University of Munich and throughout Germany realized they were almost totally dependent on the work of Jewish scholars because very few non-Jewish German scholars had studied Judaism or the history of Jews in Germany in any depth."

"So your father had that knowledge but was a political outlier as far as the Nazis were concerned?"

"He found himself between two worlds really. My father was a gentile and never part of the *Wissenschaft des Judentums* movement. At the same time he was not the kind of scholar the Nazi professors at the University were looking for. Between 1935 and 1938, they made it very difficult for him, consistently rejecting his dissertation. They believed a new type of German scholarship on Judaism and Jewish history was needed because until then it had been developed largely by Jewish historians and was inconsistent with the Nazis' antisemitic race theories. At the time, the head of the University of Munich's department of history was a Professor Karl von Muller. He knew of my father's relationship with my mother and unfairly criticized his work, telling him he'd become *verjudet*, 'judaized.'

"Professor von Muller promoted antisemitic scholars. A student roughly my father's age, Wilhelm Grau, was only twenty-four when he was awarded his PhD. Alfred Rosenberg went on to name Grau head of the Institute for Research on the Jewish Question in Frankfurt. The war began soon after my father returned from Palestine. With his academic prospects ruined he worked for a time in his father's factory, and then was called to the army. He was killed in 1943, in Yugoslavia . . ."

"Fighting Yugoslav partisans?" I interjected.

"Yes," Ruth smiled. "That much of the story Hannah told you was true.

"My grandfather, Aunt Zelda, and I started our new lives in America. We settled in Pelham Bay, where many Germans and German Jews lived. We moved into the two-bedroom apartment on Burke Avenue, and that's where I was raised, by my Aunt Zelda. I started calling her 'mutti,' which means mom in German. Zelda legally adopted me in 1945, shortly after the war ended. It took time and a lot of money because she had to get official documentation from the British authorities attesting to my mother's death in Haifa and from the American military occupation authorities confirming my father's death in 1943 while serving in the German Army. At the time she told me it all had to do with immigration requirements.

"My grandfather died in 1952; I was sixteen. Alan and I met at City College, and were married in 1958, just after graduating. We moved to Chicago because Alan had been accepted into the University of Chicago's doctoral program in economics. Hannah was born two years later. Zelda opened the hat shop after we moved. She said it was her way of honoring my grandfather."

Ruth paused for a moment and took a sip of what was by then very cold tea. "I'll have to make us some more," she said.

Chapter Twenty-Two

Ruth returned with freshly brewed tea and, after filling our cups, took a nibble of cake.

"Ruth, if you don't mind my asking," I said, "how is this all connected to Memorial Park? I'm still confused about that."

"Growing up, Hannah knew none of this. I didn't, either, until Alan and I were about to be married in 1958. Only then did my Aunt Zelda tell me the story."

"But why didn't you tell Hannah?"

"When she was growing up, Alan and I, and Zelda, felt it was best to wait. I had no close relatives in America; they never made it out of Germany and ended up in the camps. Growing up in the 1940s and early 1950s Aunt Zelda raised me. After Hannah was born and we moved back to New York, she helped me raise Hannah. Hannah grew up believing Zelda was her grandmother, because that's what we told her and who she was as a practical, and legal, matter. She heard me call Zelda mutti, and got used to calling her bubbe. Hannah loved her very much.

"Alan and I always intended to tell Hannah, first after her Bat Mitzvah, then high school, then college. It never seemed the right moment. Even when Zelda's health started to deteriorate we couldn't bring ourselves to telling Hannah because of how close she was to her bubbe. I know in retrospect it seems wrong, and it probably was. But when it looked like Zelda wasn't going to make it, I knew I had to tell Hannah.

"And so I did. I told her the whole story on Thursday, the day your letter was published in The New York Times. Neither Hannah nor I had seen it. You know I'm a devoted reader of The Times, but with Zelda in the hospital I hadn't looked at it for days. We only learned about the letter from Alan that night."

Ruth could see me bowing and shaking my head.

"Yes, that Thursday afternoon, the day before you and Hannah got together at Memorial Park."

"I can't believe this. But how could I have known?"

"You couldn't have, Michael. When I told Hannah, she was very upset, fit to be tied. She screamed that her father and I had deceived her for years. That night, after Alan came home, she started in on him, telling him that she planned to see you the next day, and had to tell you everything because she'd previously told you the false story she'd always known. Alan became irate. To be perfectly honest, he wasn't in favor of your relationship with Hannah. Without directly coming out and saying it, he was opposed to interfaith marriage and convinced that's where things were headed with the two of you."

"But your own mother and Stefan?"

"Perhaps that made it worse for him. Either way he made no secret of the fact he was opposed to your relationship. He brought up your letter, which he had read on the train coming home. The timing couldn't have been worse, I suppose. He was agitated and used your letter to tell Hannah why he didn't think you were right for her. There was a lot of talk about Israel. Alan had always been a strong supporter, but after the 1967 war his views hardened. He supported Begin's war in Lebanon, felt peace with the Arabs was not possible, that the whole world was against the Jews."

Ruth paused, "Maybe even you, he said to Hannah."

"But Hannah didn't believe that, did she? She couldn't have believed that about me. I loved her, more than anything. I wanted to spend my life with her, and would have converted if she'd wanted me to. We could have raised our . . ."

"I know how you felt, Michael, and that's why I tried to convince Alan that he was wrong about you. Hannah was always happy and fulfilled after seeing you. She would tell me for hours about the things you talked about, how you listened to her go on about all the things she loved, all those books she made you read.

"So you need to understand that when you and Hannah got together that day in Memorial Park, she was terribly upset not only about Zelda, but because of what she had learned about her real grandmother, and then the terrible argument she had with her father about you and that letter of yours."

"She argued with Alan about my letter?"

"Yes, she defended you. She said you always tried to be even-handed, to see both sides, and that's why you spoke up for the Palestinians. Hannah described it as a virtue, but Alan didn't quite see it that way.

"He reminded Hannah about our obligation to love the Jewish people, our fellow Jews." Ruth lowered her head slightly for a moment before looking up again. "He mentioned what you said at Shabbos dinner about the Palestinians, said you were an 'Arab lover,' and that since you weren't an Arab he couldn't understand why you'd ever write such a letter about Israel unless, well, unless there was something else involved."

I imagine Ruth noticed I was biting my lower lip, and the angry look in my eyes. I could accept Alan's predilection for endogamy, which was no different than my own family's, but implying to Hannah I was antisemitic because of my support for the Palestinian cause offended me deeply. Far worse in my mind was the thought that Hannah had been influenced enough by Alan to believe it. With her death, it was a question that would remain forever unanswered, as Ruth was about to acknowledge.

"I'm not telling you this to upset you, Michael, but so you can have a better understanding of what happened."

"What you're telling me is Hannah's father poisoned her mind against me."

"No, I won't say that was his intention, but I can't say it didn't have an effect on Hannah, I'm afraid. It all started at that Shabbos dinner, if you remember."

"I try to forget that night," I replied, quickly adding, "except for your kugel of course."

Ruth let out a laugh, the only one she'd had for a while, she said.

"So I assume that after I brought Hannah home that day she told you and Alan everything that happened between us?"

"Yes, and not surprisingly, Hannah's father saw it as vindication of the views he'd expressed the night before. But Zelda's condition worsened over the weekend and she passed away the following Wednesday, so that sort of took things over."

"I still don't understand what led Hannah to suddenly go to Israel?"

"The December trip was Alan's idea and he came up with it somewhat out of the blue, right after Hannah's birthday and your day with her at the Cloisters. Now I have my thoughts about my husband's timing, but Hannah did fall in love with Israel. Then, with what she learned about my mother's passion for Zionism, she felt she had to explore it all more deeply, find out what it was about Israel and Zionism that had motivated her grandmother. You know the way she was, when she read a book she would go back and re-read whole chapters to dig deeper and deeper, always searching for the meaning. It was the same with the story of her grandmother. She found it a mystery, a fascinating mystery that she needed to figure out. The last few years she'd been writing a book about her grandmother and my Aunt Zelda, trying to make sense of it all."

"The search becomes the meaning," I whispered to myself.

"What was that?"

"Nothing, just something Hannah said to me once."

"With Zelda's passing and her discovery of my mother's story, she felt this incredible curiosity pulling at her, the need to search for 'the real Hanna,' she said, to understand what compelled her to go to Palestine, to make the decision to stay even though it meant giving me up, then later to take her own life.

She saw it as such a tragic story. How could I disagree? After classes ended, Hannah decided to visit Israel. Hannah's father encouraged her, and so did I, at least at the time just for the summer. It was so important to her."

"Why didn't she share any of this with me? I would have understood. Why wouldn't she meet me when she first heard I was in Israel?"

"I don't know why she never shared with you what she learned about my mother, or her feelings about moving to Israel. That's a question I can't answer. What I know is that when I asked if she'd spoken to you about everything she said no, it wasn't the right time. Maybe it was her father insisting she shouldn't reveal our family secret. Maybe it was the tension between you and him, and Hannah's not wanting to go against her father's wishes. I honestly don't know.

"But she didn't refuse to meet you. When I spoke to Hannah, she was stunned to hear you were in Israel. She did everything but accuse me of plotting the whole thing and, well, she might have had a point. But she needed more time to think, and said she'd call me back. She wasn't in Jerusalem. She was in Haifa. She had visited the cemetery where my mother is buried, and was searching for the places where she had lived from 1936 to 1941, researching to see if there was anyone still alive who might have known my mother. She'd made me give her all the names and information before she left, translate the letters, everything.

"After I talked to her, you called. Perhaps I could have been clearer, more direct when we spoke. I was hoping you'd be patient. Hannah was very confused about her feelings for you, and wasn't sure what to do about meeting you. But she asked me to find out where you were, and promised to call me back, once she figured something out. That's why I asked you all those questions. Do you remember?"

"I remember everything, Ruth" I said, wearily.

"When she got back to me after you called that night from Tel Aviv, I gave her the name of the hotel, Paradise or something, and the address you told me. She went there the next morning from Haifa. She had to take two or three buses. It's sixty miles away. She understood you'd be in Tel Aviv till Saturday because that's what you told me, and she thought you knew she'd be going there the next morning. She said she called the hotel to tell you, but the reception person who answered said you'd gone out. He must not have given you Hannah's message."

"No, no, he didn't. I'm not sure what to say, Ruth. This is a lot to absorb."

"I know this is difficult, Michael. But with Hannah gone I felt you should know everything. That it was important for you to understand."

"Hannah said once we aren't supposed to understand everything. I still don't understand why she decided to make aliyah without talking to me, without our discussing it together. I guess by then she'd decided she didn't want me to be a part of her life, not her new life at least."

"I can tell you that Hannah's summer in Israel and her grandmother's story had a powerful impact on her. I can't tell you it didn't change the way she felt about you. That may not be what you want to hear. So I don't have the answer to your question, and won't pretend to tell you what was in Hannah's heart, whether or how her feelings for you changed over time or what may have changed them. But I know she cared for you. Still, there will always be things we don't know, that neither of us will ever understand. I've given you some answers today, but I don't have all of them. And you have to come to grips with the fact that you never will."

"That's what she wrote, she 'cared about me' and 'missed our friendship.'" The tone of my voice almost certainly betrayed the bitterness I still harbored after seven years. Ruth looked at me intently.

"For some people, Michael, the passion generated by an idea may be the most powerful force of all, more powerful than anything else, maybe even love."

We both fell silent for a long moment.

"Ruth," I said finally, "I know how hard this has been for you, especially with your having lost Alan too. It's getting late and I won't stay. I want you to know how grateful I am for your calling, for telling me about Hannah, and for everything you've shared today. I'll never forget it. But before I go, there's one more thing. I'd like to visit Hannah's grave in Israel. Can you give me the details of where she is?"

"Oh, Michael, I couldn't ask or expect you to do that."

"You're not asking me, at least not this time."

Ruth paused for a moment. "Well, I wouldn't try talking you out of it then. Let me get that for you."

Ruth exited the room and walked up the stairs. She returned a few minutes later with a business-sized envelope that she said contained a map describing the location of the Haifa cemetery where Hannah had been buried. Along with the envelope, Ruth handed me a brochure from the Cloisters.

"After Hannah died, I was going through her boxes in the basement and came across this."

Hannah had saved the brochure from our visit eight years before. I opened and began to peruse it, moving my hand up and down the richly textured paper, thinking, and hoping, that Hannah had kept it as a reminder of how much we'd once meant to each other. In the right hand corner of one of the pages, just opposite a photograph of the Cuxa courtyard, she'd written "Hannah" alongside "Michael" and the date. She'd drawn a heart around our names.

"That was a special day for me," I said, shaken by what I'd seen.

"And for Hannah. She talked to me for hours about it."

"Thank you, Ruth. You don't know how much this means to me."

"I think, Michael, maybe I do," Ruth replied.

I stood to say goodbye and Ruth walked me to the door. We hugged for a long time, and promised each other we'd stay in touch.

Over the next three decades Ruth and I remained friends and kept in contact through calls, visits, and letters. Ruth preferred "pen to paper" letters, a "lost art" she would say, and she shunned email when it came into widespread use. It was during my last visit with Ruth, shortly before her death a few months ago, that I again saw little Ruth, Hannah's daughter, who I had first met thirty years before. She was married and living in New York, with children of her own. Her father, Matt, who'd remarried four years after Hannah's death, and her brother, Joshua, still lived in Israel.

"After Hannah died, I spent more than a month in Israel, for Shiva and the mourning period," Ruth told me as I departed. "And I'm planning to go back soon to spend time with Matt and my grandchildren, but I don't know when that'll be. In the meantime, Michael, place a stone on her grave for me, please."

"Yours will be the first," I promised Ruth.

Chapter Twenty-Three

Two weeks after that day with Ruth, the school year ended at Xavier and I was, so to speak, a free man. I'd already booked my flight to Israel and departed on Tuesday evening, following the prior weekend's graduation ceremony.

I planned to stay only three days. Given the short duration of the trip the airfare was astronomical, but I didn't care. I felt the need to visit Hannah's grave, for her, for me, and, perhaps most of all, for Ruth. It seemed the least I could do after she had been thoughtful enough to tell me about Hannah and share her painful story.

I didn't think it appropriate to visit Israel without expressing condolences to Hannah's husband. And, to be honest, there was also an element of curiosity in my wanting to meet him. I called Ruth and asked if she could first contact Matt to find out whether he'd be willing to see me. Matt told her he would. When I called him to set up a date and time, he said he couldn't be available until Thursday evening. Once our meeting had been arranged, I decided to spend a day in Jerusalem, then travel on to Haifa to visit Matt and, on Friday morning, go to the cemetery where Hannah was buried, before returning to New York the next day.

After arriving in Israel, I made my way by bus to East Jerusalem, where I had booked a room at the Palestinian, family-run hotel I'd stayed at seven years before, a converted nineteenth-century Arab mansion not far from the Damascus Gate. I told Khaled, the loquacious and now-balding proprietor, that I remembered my earlier stay fondly and that he was the reason I'd returned. He replied with a hearty laugh and said he remembered me also, although I doubted he really did. Khaled spoke pridefully and at length about how his grandfather, his father, and he had operated the hotel for decades, and how generations of his family had lived in East Jerusalem, which Israel annexed in 1980. He pointed to his son, Yousef, working a short distance away, and told me he would manage the hotel in the future. Khaled had told me the same story, nearly word for word, seven years earlier.

As Khaled spoke I saw Yousef nearby, tending to some of the large, leafy plants arranged around the perimeter of the hotel's foyer. Yousef was a handsome young man in his early-twenties, with neatly cropped hair and deep, penetrating eyes. When I'd last seen him, he was a mischievous teen playing with his sisters in the hotel garden. As he walked over to greet me, I noticed his right forearm and hand bandaged with gauze. Wondering how he had gotten injured, I asked about the Intifada, the series of then ongoing and often violent protests against Israel's occupation that had first erupted in 1987. Only a few days before leaving New York, I'd read about Israel's practice of "breaking the bones" of stone-throwing Palestinians. But as soon as Yousef began describing a protest that had taken place recently not far from the hotel, implying he had been a part of it, Khaled rushed over and interrupted us.

"*La, la,*"—"no, no," he said with urgency, first in Arabic and then repeating himself in English. "There is no problem here. We have only a quiet business. No troubles. Please." I took Khaled's cue and promptly changed the subject. I asked him if he could recommend something for me to do that afternoon, and he referred me to a Christian tour company, kindly offering to call the operators to reserve a spot for me on the afternoon tour of Jericho. The tour bus stopped regularly in front of the hotel to pick up his guests, Khaled told me. I agreed and thanked him.

Less than an hour later, I went on a short excursion to Jericho organized by the group Khaled recommended. As our bus wound its way through the occupied West Bank, we drove past the Jewish settlement of Ma'ale Adumim and deep into the Judean desert as it descends to the Dead Sea, down to Tel es-Sultan, the site of ancient Jericho, the world's oldest city. After viewing the stunning remains of the city's watchtower and listening to our guide retell the biblical tale of Joshua, he drove us to a point close to Qasr al-Yahud, located just southeast of Jericho, a tourist site on the western bank of the Jordan River linked to John the Baptist. Previously operated by the Jordanians, the site had been closed since the Six-Day War. The guide explained that al-Maghtas—"Bethany beyond the Jordan," located on the opposite, eastern bank of the river just across from Qasr al-Yahud—was the traditional spot where Jesus was thought to have been baptized. It was there, the guide said, quoting the Gospel of John, that God proclaimed, "This is my beloved son, in whom I am well pleased." Against the din raised by professions of awe and whirling camera clicks, I wished silently that I had the faith to believe it.

Following my return, I spent a lonely night roaming the darkened, narrow streets of the Old City, recreating as best I could the route I'd taken along the Via Dolorossa seven years earlier. I stopped for kosher pizza, which Hannah had first introduced me to in New York, and later, on my way back to the hotel, for dark, rich Arab coffee and sweet *knafeh*, a Palestinian pastry.

On Thursday, I bid farewell to Khaled and Yousef and made my way to Haifa, a bustling city on the coast with a mixed population of Israelis and Palestinians. I spent a few hours in the late-afternoon walking the boulevards of the shopping districts, and then down to the promenade overlooking the port and crystal-blue Mediterranean Sea. Early that evening, following dinner alone at my hotel, I took a taxi up to Kiryat Yam, a sedate suburb of Haifa a few miles north of the city.

The taxi dropped me off on a quiet street lined with four-story apartment buildings, in what seemed like a middle class neighborhood. Kiryat Yam was a beach town, the driver told me, which made sense knowing how much Hannah had enjoyed the Jersey shore. After a few knocks, Matt answered, complimenting me on my punctuality, something rare in Israel, he said. Thin with blond hair, several inches taller than me, and wearing wire-rimmed glasses that matched my own, Matt was gracious and introduced me to his son Joshua and little Ruth, who, in the Jewish tradition, had been named after her grandmother. Prodded by Matt, Joshua offered me a shy smile and shook my outstretched hand, but Ruth clung to her father's side, hugging his leg tenaciously and refusing to let go until coaxed by Joshua's invitation to play.

The apartment had a bright, airy feel, with an open floor plan, the kitchen leading into a small dining area that blended seamlessly with the living room. As Matt excused himself to get each of us orange sodas, my eyes darted around the apartment. There were photos of Hannah, Matt, and the kids, of Ruth and Alan, and another couple I later confirmed were Matt's parents. I took note of the style of the furniture, which I presumed Hannah had picked out, along with the books and knick-knacks on the wall shelves, all the accoutrements of average life that we accumulate over time. But they provided no window into Hannah's life with Matt in Israel, no revelations that held any discernible meaning for me.

I found speaking with Matt awkward, as one might expect, and assumed he felt the same. Hannah had told him about me years earlier, Matt said, so he was aware of the circumstances under which our relationship had ended. At first Matt tried his best to put me at ease. He talked about his childhood in Rochester, his college years at Carnegie-Mellon, and about starting his new life in Israel after making aliyah and serving in the Israeli army.

Although Matt politely answered all of my questions about Hannah and the children, he several times shifted the conversation abruptly, asking me about sports and politics in America. I certainly couldn't blame him for not wanting to discuss Hannah with an old romance a mere four months after she'd been killed in a car accident. And I had no right to expect anything more of him. Hannah and I had dated for about a year seven years before. The relationship had ended when she decided I wasn't the person she wanted to spend her life with, and we both had moved on. Was it any more complicated than that, I asked myself. I started to feel like I had that night in Dizengoff Square with Dan and Eitan, an intruder in a stranger's house, trespassing where I didn't belong.

I told Matt I had best be going since he had his hands full getting the kids settled and off to bed. Matt said he had arranged for a sitter, but she'd canceled on him unexpectedly only late that afternoon. I honestly couldn't imagine how he was going to handle the situation, but he said Hannah and he had a strong circle of friends, and that his parents as well as Ruth were planning to come to Israel and spend time with him, perhaps a month or two. He'd manage somehow, he said. It was Joshua and Ruth he was worried about.

The pair was running around screaming like kids do at that age, with Matt barking haplessly at them in a mixture of Hebrew and English. It was neither the time nor place for me to seek answers as to why Hannah had given "all her heart" to Matt, but refused the offer of my own. I'd lost Hannah seven years before; Matt's loss was incomparably greater as he and Hannah had built a life together, one tragically cut short. They had fulfilled their shared dream of making aliyah to Israel, and produced two beautiful children. I felt only sadness for him, for her, and for them.

Just before leaving, I turned to Matt and said, "If you don't mind one more question, Matt. You made aliyah around the same time as Hannah. Can you tell me why? What made you decide to come here, to leave your life and family in America?" He turned his head upward, and made a sweeping motion across his mouth with his right hand.

"You can call it ideology, I suppose, but without getting into all the politics of it, I believe that Jews are at home here in Israel." Although making aliyah "might not be the right choice for all Jews," Matt said, it had been for him. Once he'd concluded it was part of his "personal destiny," he "felt compelled." He didn't "mean to be dramatic," but explained he wasn't exaggerating the emotions he'd experienced ten years earlier. "To be honest," Matt said, reminding me of what Hannah told me years before in Memorial Park, "I'm not sure you can fully understand this if you're not Jewish.

"Hannah felt the same way," he continued after a pause. "It's what drew us to each other when we first met. She never regretted her decision to come here, if that's what you're really asking."

"No," I said, "I never doubted for a minute that she felt the same."

I turned and moved toward the front door, preparing to leave.

"Michael, wait," Matt said suddenly, before disappearing into one of the back rooms. When he returned a minute later, he was holding what appeared to be a bound manuscript. He handed it to me.

"What's this?" I asked.

"It's the book Hannah was writing about her grandmother. Ruth tells me you know the whole story now. Hannah worked on it for years, even learned to read German and went to Munich twice to do research. But she never finished it. She told me she was sure you'd be interested in reading it, something about the 'stories within history,' she said. I think she would've wanted you to have a copy."

I opened the cover and glanced at the title page, *Searching for Hanna*.

After a silent moment passed between us, Matt placed his hands gently on top of mine. "Let me know what you think," he said. "Now, I've got to get these kids to bed."

I thanked Matt for sharing Hannah's book with me, and again for agreeing to meet under such difficult circumstances. We shook hands and embraced. Holding the manuscript tightly against my chest, I walked down the quiet street until I found a taxi stand at the spot Matt had suggested I would, and returned to my hotel in Haifa. I stayed up reading

Hannah's book until it was nearly dawn, and then, chased by specters of the past I could not otherwise outrun, fell into a deep and soundless sleep.

Chapter Twenty-Four

"Our memory is a more perfect world than the universe: it gives back life to those who no longer exist."

Guy de Maupassant

By mid-morning, I was in a taxi on my way to Hof Ha Karmel, the cemetery where Hannah's grandmother was buried. After leaving Ruth's house a few weeks before, I noticed that together with the map and papers about Hannah's grave, Ruth had given me, inadvertently or not I couldn't be sure, a map of the cemetery indicating where her mother was. Perhaps Ruth hadn't felt comfortable asking me to visit her mother's grave, but before leaving for Israel I called to let her know I planned to.

Stepping out in front of the iron entrance gate, I put on the kippah I had bought after arriving at Ben Gurion Airport. One of the attendants told me that the cemetery was established in 1937, after the Old Cemetery of Haifa had filled up. I followed his initial directions, then used Ruth's map, which was marked up with arrows, lines, and circles. After a few missteps, I came upon the gravestone of "Johanna Reiner née Manzbach," covered with green moss and tilted to the right by several inches, the first name written in the formal German spelling and appearing just below the Hebrew letters.

I marveled at the life of the diminutive yet determined woman whose photograph Ruth had shown me in New Jersey, and whose very existence I had been unaware of three weeks before. Hanna Manzbach affected the lives of so many people who had, in turn, affected my own: Walter Manzbach, Zelda, Stefan, Ruth, Hannah, and through Hannah, me. Had Hannah not heard her tragic story would she be lying in a grave a few miles away—her life cut short at the same age as her ill-fated grandmother, each devoured by the insentient maw of history—or thousands of miles away in New York, still wrapped in my arms? I could never know. Perhaps, as Ruth had said, it was all *beshert*, meant to be.

I found two jagged rocks, placed them on top of the gravestone, and left.

The cemetery where Hannah was buried—Sde Yehoshua—was fairly close, and I was able quickly to get an Egged bus that dropped me off at the front gate. During the ride I thought about the Jewish tradition of placing stones on graves. As I understood it, unlike flowers that wither and die, the stone represents the permanence of our memory of the dead, and a bond between us and them. The Hebrew word for pebble, tz'ror, means "to bond," and, for that reason, many gravestones have engraved on them the words "tz'ror haHayyim," meaning, for a woman, "Let her soul be bound up in the bond of eternal life." I found the age-old practice, especially its connection to memory, moving and life-affirming.

Arriving at the cemetery, I followed Ruth's carefully marked map and, after about a ten-minute search, came upon Hannah's grave. I shuddered at the initial, surreal sight of the raised, new white marble slab lying flat against the earth, a small headstone with engraved lettering resting at its top like a pillow. A moment later, remembering my promise to Ruth, I picked up two smooth stones, one for her, one for me. I whispered Ruth's name and set the first one down just below the headstone, then placed the second alongside the first.

I stood over Hannah's grave in silence, without uttering any prayer; there was no god I believed in from whom I could beseech benediction for Hannah, or seek solace for myself. Ruth had told me that ideology might be the most powerful force in the world, more powerful perhaps than love. I understood why she, and I, might have felt that way. I'd reached the same conclusion that night in Dizengoff Square seven years before. But I had since concluded that memory is, because it endures long after time tempers the passions of both ideology and the heart's love. It had been the magnetic and lasting power of remembrance—individual, collective, and historical—that compelled Hannah to go off in search of her grandmother's "story within history." After reading Hannah's manuscript and meeting Matt and their children, I was convinced Hannah's search had led her back to herself, and that my own had finally come to an end.

I was convinced, too, that Paul had been wrong about the resurrection of the dead. The dead live on, but only in the minds of those who remember them. It is memory that enables us to invert time and navigate between the present moment and the world of our past, where death is without power to deny us reunion with those we have loved. And with equally irresistible force it is memory that prevents us from forgetting them, perpetuating the pain of their loss and ensuring that our wounds chafe, fester, and never fully heal. I had neither seen nor spoken to Hannah in seven years, yet during that time, and even through death, my memory of her continued to mediate between us, to haunt and wield power over me. I was determined to break its spell if I could.

I took from my knapsack the music box I had planned to give Hannah at The Sign of the Dove to celebrate the one-year anniversary of our meeting again at Princeton. It played the serenade from Eine

Klein Nachtmusik, her favorite, as a figurine of Mozart spun around atop a piano. I wound the key as far as it could go, and placed the box near the marble headstone just as a warm breeze arose and encircled me. I listened as the chimes were carried along with the wind, their melody at first fast and furious, reminiscent of Hannah and me in the beginning, then slower and slower still, until the final note lingered in the air like a long, last kiss goodbye, and the chimes fell silent.

Chapter Twenty-Five

I arrived in New York late afternoon the following day, and took a taxi from JFK into Manhattan. I stopped in the apartment to drop off my small bag and, although exhausted from the trip, decided on a walk in Riverside Park to clear my mind. I had a lot of thinking to do, and decisions to make, in the days ahead. I would need to find another teaching job, and quickly, as it was already July. I'd have to start writing letters and checking school listings for last-minute openings.

I called Pat to let him know I was back. I told him I was considering getting the certification needed to teach history in public school, rather than continuing with the Catholic school system I'd been in for four years. He reminded me that even Brennan had said he thought me better suited to teach in the public schools when he offered to write me a letter of recommendation the day he fired me.

I'd also been thinking about a new apartment, I said. Dick was planning to retire, and he and Iris had pretty much moved permanently to the country house. But they were happy for me to stay on because they didn't plan to give up their apartment in the city as it came in handy whenever they wanted to take in a Broadway show or concert at Lincoln Center. I could have full use of the second bedroom and essentially run of the place, but I was determined that once I found a new job I would find a new apartment as well. Pat thought it was a good idea.

"And what about Estrella?" Pat asked. "Is she working tonight?"

"Not sure. Sometimes she takes off on the weekends," I replied.

"Well, you do have to eat."

~~~

The day had been sunny and calm, although scorchingly hot, and now an evening thunderstorm was brewing. Walking back toward Broadway, I got caught in the storm and was soaked to the skin by the time it was over.

I decided to stop at Dimitri's for dinner. The old red leather booth—right side of the double row, second in from the front—was occupied by a young couple whispering to each other and holding hands across the center of the table. I was still dripping wet from the torrential rain and about to head over to the counter when Estrella noticed me waiting near the entrance and led me to a table up front overlooking Broadway.

Following closely behind, I sensed something different. Estrella's lustrous black hair, usually pulled tight and into a bun, was loose that night, flowing freely and alluringly down her back. She handed me one of those laminated, oversized menus and I began to peruse it, pretending to be musing over the choices when I already knew what I wanted.

After a moment, Estrella exhaled in feigned exasperation, then turned her head slightly downward and said jokingly in a fake Spanish accent, "Miguel, you look like hell."

"Seriously, amigo," she continued before I could say anything, "where have you been? You're all beat up. You sure you want your hot tea with lemon? Maybe you could use something different tonight, like a strong cup of Spanish coffee, specialty of the house?"

"I'll stick with tea for now," I said, as Estrella's bright and cheerful eyes met my dark, sullen ones. "But how about that drink I promised you?"

"I get off at nine, so I'll meet you out front," Estrella replied matter-of-factly, with a smile. Then she winked at me, just like she always did.

Made in United States
North Haven, CT
26 April 2022